PUFFIN BOOKS

LITTLE
BADMAN
AND THE
INVASION
OF THE
KILLER
AUNTIES

LITTLE BADMAN

AND THE
INVASION OF THE KILLER AUNTIES

HUMZA ARSHAD & HENRY WHITE

Illustrated by ALEKSEI BITSKOFF

PUFFIN

PUFFIN BOOKS

UK | USA | Canada | Ireland | Australia
India | New Zealand | South Africa

Puffin Books is part of the Penguin Random House group of companies
whose addresses can be found at global.penguinrandomhouse.com.

www.penguin.co.uk
www.puffin.co.uk
www.ladybird.co.uk

Penguin
Random House
UK

First published 2019

005

Text copyright © Big Deal Films Ltd, 2019
Illustrations copyright © Aleksei Bitskoff, 2019

BIG DEAL FILMS

The moral right of the author and illustrator has been asserted

Set in 13/18pt Bembo

Printed in Great Britain by Clays Ltd, Elcograf S.p.A.

A CIP catalogue record for this book is available from the British Library

ISBN: 978–0–241–34060–8

All correspondence to:
Puffin Books
Penguin Random House Children's
80 Strand, London WC2R 0RL

MIX
Paper from
responsible sources
FSC® C018179
www.fsc.org FSC

Penguin Random House is committed to a
sustainable future for our business, our readers
and our planet. This book is made from Forest
Stewardship Council® certified paper.

To my mum and dad, my family, my three-and-a-half fans (I may have more but that's just an estimate) and, most importantly, to God – Humza

For Ellen, who read with me – Henry

CHAPTER ONE
A BEE NAMED MUSTAFA

You've probably heard of me, right? Little Badman. No? Oh. Well. . . Doesn't matter. You will do one day. I'm gonna be big. And not like my Uncle Abdul, who ate his own bodyweight in samosas and ended up in hospital. The good kind of big. Rich, famous and respected. Like Jay-Z, or that old white man from KFC.

I was always destined to be big. Even when I was born my mum said it was like trying to fit a nappy on a dishwasher. I call it big boned. Whatever. Point is, I'm a big fish in a small pond. Like a shark in a fish bowl, or a pit bull in a hamster cage. Sooner or later, I'm gonna explode out of there and the world is gonna know my name. Humza Khan.

But you can call me Little Badman.

My path to greatness wasn't always clear. Even a ninja-rapper-gangster like me has to start somewhere. And I started in the hood. Proper gangland territory: the Little Meadows Primary School, Eggington. To say there was a lot of gun crime would be an understatement. There was loads. Just not in Eggington. Mostly in America, I think. Still, I reckon it shaped me into the twelve-year-old I am today.

But nothing, and I mean nothing, shaped me as much as my final year at primary school. I don't know if you've ever seen any war movies, about Vietnam or Iraq or the Galactic Empire, but none of that compares to what I went through in my final year at school. To call myself the greatest hero the world has ever known would be arrogant, so I won't do that. I'll leave you all to form your own opinion once you get to the end of my tale.

And, like so many of history's greatest conflicts, it all began with something so small. In my case, it was a bee named Mustafa . . .

I was sitting in class next to Umer, when his pencil case started to vibrate.

'Is it me or is your pencil case ringing?' I asked, watching the little metal box rattle along the desk.

'Nah, that's just my bee,' replied Umer. 'He's always doing that.'

'Why've you got a bee in your pencil case, man? Let that bee go!'

'No way,' Umer said, trying carefully to peer inside the lid without the bee escaping. 'I'm keeping him. I've never had a pet before.'

'A bee ain't a pet. You can't stroke a bee or teach it tricks. A bee's a bee.'

'Doesn't mean it can't be a pet,' said Umer. 'My cousin had a worm named Liam.'

'Yeah, well, at least a worm ain't gonna sting you.'

'Mustafa wouldn't sting me.'

'Who the hell is Mustafa?'

'My bee,' replied Umer.

'You called your bee Mustafa?'

'Yeah, Mustafa Bee.'

'Why?'

'Because I . . . *must-av-a bee.*'

'I don't even know why we're friends, man.'

See, this is the kind of thing I have to put up with. I'm not saying Umer's an idiot, but you can only watch someone put their shoes on the wrong feet so many times before you start to wonder. Still, he *is* my best friend. Not forever, obviously. When I'm a famous ninja-rapper I'll probably be best friends with Busta Rhymes or Dr Dre, or one of the Power Rangers. But, for now, I've got to put up with Umer.

'Ow!' shouted Umer, slamming the pencil case shut.

'Did you just get stung?' I asked.

'No,' replied Umer, rubbing his swollen thumb. 'Well . . . maybe.'

'Oh great,' I said. 'Now you've killed him.'

'"Killed him"?' gasped Umer, staring at the pencil case containing his bee. 'What are you talking about? I haven't touched him!'

'You don't have to. Once they sting you, that's it – they die.'

'What? I didn't know that!' cried Umer. 'Why did you do it, Mustafa? Why?'

'Quiet down, man – we're gonna get in trouble.'

'Oh, Mustafa! Why?' wailed Umer, tears filling his eyes.

'You two!' came a voice from the front of the class. 'What's going on back there?'

'Uh, nothing, miss,' I replied. 'Umer just got stung by a bee.'

'He's dying, miss! He's dying!' bawled Umer.

'Who's dying?' said Miss Crumble, sounding panicked.

'Mustafa!' replied Umer.

'Who on earth is Mustafa?' asked Miss Crumble, arriving at the desk.

'My bee! My poor dead bee!'

'A bee?' she said, looking a little nervous and taking a step back. 'You're sure he's dead?'

'He's a goner, miss,' I replied. 'Umer basically murdered him.'

'I didn't mean to!' wailed Umer.

'OK, as long as you're certain he's dead,' she said, looking relieved.

'I'm afraid so, miss,' I replied, shaking my head. 'He's buzzed his last buzz. Gone to the great beehive in the sky. He's making honey for Tupac.'

'For goodness' sake,' muttered Miss Crumble. 'It's always something with you two, isn't it?'

'Don't blame me,' I replied. 'Blame Mr Bee-keeper here.'

'Hey, look!' Umer beamed, looking up from the open pencil case. 'He's not dead after all!'

Now it wasn't long after that that I learned some important lessons about bees. Firstly, not all bees die after they sting you – turns out that's just honeybees. Secondly, big hairy Mustafa was actually a bumblebee and had no intention of dying anytime soon. And thirdly (and this one was probably most important of all), Miss Crumble is, and always has been, super allergic to bee-stings. Like crazy, serious, life-threatening allergic. Oops.

Miss Crumble let out a scream so loud and horrible that Wendy Wang's glasses shattered right there on her face. Miss C began to flail her arms around like a windmill in a hurricane, desperately trying to swat poor Mustafa.

'Calm down, miss,' I said. 'It's only a bee.'

But Miss Crumble wasn't listening. She was in a wild panic. No one in the class was laughing, because none of us could decide if this was hilarious or actually a bit scary. I mean, seriously, she looked insane. She was knocking over desks, pulling posters off the walls, spinning around so fast I felt dizzy just watching her. And then the inevitable happened. You can only imprison an innocent bee for so long before he cracks. And Mustafa had had enough.

Flying between Miss Crumble's windmilling fists, Mustafa scored a direct hit, right on the end of her nose. Pow! You could almost hear the sting popping into that big red veiny target. Miss Crumble froze instantly. She stopped screaming, stopped swinging her arms. She just looked at the end of her nose until she went fully cross-eyed. Mustafa looked right back at her. He wiggled his bum, gave a short victorious buzz and then flew out the window.

'Bye, Mustafa,' said Umer, waving. 'I'll never forget you.'

Miss Crumble still didn't move an inch – except for her nose, which was already growing at an alarming rate. It was like someone was inflating a balloon in there. In an instant the swelling had spread to her cheeks, her neck, her hands.

She plonked down in her chair, looking dazed.

'Mnnnggg nugg unggg,' she said, which I think roughly translates as: *my tongue has swollen*.

'Huh,' I said, watching her slowly inflate. 'Do you reckon she's gonna burst?'

'I hope not,' replied Umer. 'Maybe we should go get some help?'

'I dunno. She's had a pretty good innings.'

'Humza!'

'Yeah, yeah, OK,' I said, pushing my seat out. 'I mean, if you felt that bad about killing a bee, imagine how you're gonna feel after killing a teacher.'

'Humza!' cried Umer, who was starting to look a bit ill himself.

'Only playing, man. Come on – let's go save the day.'

And with that we jumped up and ran off to look for a teacher who wasn't about to explode.

When the ambulance took her away, Miss Crumble looked like a beach ball dressed as a woman. I couldn't help but feel like maybe I was just a tiny little bit responsible. After all, I was the one who had assured her Mustafa was dead. But, in my defence, if there are gaps in my knowledge about bees, who could be more responsible than my own teacher? So really, when you take that into account, it was all Miss Crumble's fault and I'm totally blameless. I felt much better after that.

'Come on, Umer,' I said. 'Let's go shoot some more scenes for the video.'

'I don't know, Humza. Aren't we meant to be in a lesson?'

'How we gonna go to a lesson when the teacher's dead?'

'Dead?' said Umer, looking shocked.

'Or sick, I don't know. I ain't a doctor. Now come on – if we're quick, we can film the whole chorus before lunch.'

'Not so fast, you two,' came a booming voice from nearby.

'Uh-oh,' said Umer, swallowing so hard you could hear it.

Before we could even turn round, a large hairy hand fell on each of our shoulders.

'What's this I hear about you two and Miss Crumble?' asked Mr Offalbox.

Now I don't know what your headmaster's like, but ours was big. King Kong big. Like a Volvo in a tie. Have you ever seen one of those cop shows on TV where there's a really angry sergeant? Well, ours looked like the sergeant that ate that sergeant. He had this huge moustache, like the head of a broom, that stretched and contracted like a caterpillar when he spoke. His head alone must have weighed the same as my sofa. He was not someone you wanted to get on the wrong side of.

'Uh, I can explain!' I said as fast as I could get the words out.

'No need for that, Humza,' said Mr Offalbox. 'The paramedics explained everything.'

Uh-oh. I had a sinking feeling I was about to get it, and get it bad. And, however bad Mr Offalbox could be, it wouldn't come close to the trouble I'd be in when my mum and dad found out. No one punishes like a Pakistani parent. They take courses in it. Evening classes on the subject of making their kids suffer. So, at this point, I figured I might just have to run away and join the circus. Or the Mafia. Whichever was easier to get into. And then something unexpected happened.

'You boys are heroes!' said Mr Offalbox. 'They

say that without your quick thinking Miss Crumble might well have died. Well done, the pair of you!'

'Oh, right,' I said with a smile. 'Yeah, I was about to say the same thing.'

'Did they explain about Mustafa?' asked Umer, before I could elbow him in the ribs.

'*Shut up about Mustafa!*' I hissed, then added a little louder: 'What he means is, did they mention that we *must-have-a* reward for our bravery?'

'Well, no, they didn't,' said Mr Offalbox. 'But, now you mention it, I think that's a very good idea.'

'How about half a day off for good behaviour?' I suggested.

'HA HA HA!' roared Mr Offalbox, leaning back with his hands on his hips. 'Of course not! But I think I might just be able to convince the dinner ladies to give you a second helping of dessert.'

'Yeah, good luck with that,' I replied. 'Those old girls are strict as. Have you even seen the healthy stuff they make us eat these days? I swear I'm turning into a rabbit.'

'Just you leave it to me, Humza. I know a thing or two about charming dinner ladies,' he said with a wink, and turned to walk away.

'Urgh,' I said to Umer after he'd gone. 'Old

people shouldn't wink. I just swallowed some sick.'

'Still, double dessert. That's not a bad result,' he replied.

'Yeah, maybe we should nearly kill teachers more often!'

'Hmm, I don't know. One's probably enough for me.'

'Fair enough. Come on, then – let's go film that shot.'

See, school is just a place I go to every day. Sort of like prison, but with worse food. My *real* work is making the greatest rap music video ever produced. How else am I expected to become so famous that people fight wars over me? I'm gonna be so big Little Badman Impersonator will be a valid career choice. I'm gonna be so popular that cats'll learn to speak just to ask me for selfies. I'm gonna be so rich that even my butler's butler will have a butler. And the only way to do any of that is to make myself a smash-hit music video. Enter my cameraman, Umer.

Now, Umer may not have a lot of media training, and he might be shooting on his dad's old Nokia from the Stone Age, and he may shake quite a lot when he's nervous, but, all of that aside, he's got a pretty good eye. And, more importantly, he's the only one I can get to do the job. But it shouldn't matter too much – after all, when you're pointing the camera at me, it's hard to go wrong.

'Uh, Humza,' said Umer ten minutes later, while looking through the tiny screen on his phone. 'I don't know how gangsta this feels.'

'What do you mean?'

'Well . , . it kind of looks like you're in a toilet. At a primary school.'

'Really? How can you tell?'

'Probably the little urinals. They're a bit of a giveaway.'

'Hmm. That ain't ideal. But it's the best we're gonna do. Can you frame them out?'

'Maybe, but I'm trying not to show too much of the graffiti.'

'Why? We did that specially.'

'Well, it's just that it doesn't look very real. You can tell we've done it on paper and stuck it to the walls.'

'Of course we have. We don't want to get in trouble, do we?' I said.

'Yeah, no, of course. But, you know, that's the bit that's not very gangsta.'

'I see what you're saying. Real rappers don't worry about getting detention. OK, just show a bit of the toilets and a bit of the graffiti. People are mostly gonna be looking at me anyway.'

'Got it,' said Umer, and hit RECORD.

I took a deep breath and pulled my best gangsta face (basically you just squint a little and look like you've never smiled for a photo in your life). Then I started spitting my rhymes:

'B to the A to the D to the Man,
If other rappers can't, Little Badman can.
Straight from the hood like a rat from a drain,
Rhymes so sick they're melting your brain.'

That was as far as I got before the door to the toilet burst open.

'There you are!' snarled Mr Offalbox. Even with just his head peering round the door he seemed huge. Maybe the tiny urinals added to the illusion. It looked like the giant in Jack and the Beanstalk had stopped by for a wee. We had nowhere to run. And that was when I spotted her: Wendy Wang, peering round the door beside the headmaster. Of course! Classic Wendy Wang. She just couldn't keep it to herself.

'Wendy here says,' began Mr Offalbox, 'that perhaps you two aren't the heroes I took you for. Is that so?'

'Define "heroes",' I replied.

'She says it was you two who got Miss Crumble stung in the first place, that you'd been tormenting that bee and then lied about it being deceased.'

'How would Wendy Wang know? She hasn't even got her glasses on.'

'That's your fault too!' said Wendy, before hiding a little further behind the door.

'Humza, imagine you were me,' continued Mr Offalbox.

'I don't know if my imagination's big enough, sir,' I replied.

'Shut up, boy,' he muttered. 'Now, if you were me and you received one side of a story from top student, class president and chess-team captain Wendy Wang, and a very different, contradictory story from D-student, class clown and boy voted most likely to get caught in a bear trap Humza Khan, who would *you* believe?'

'Definitely the bear-trap guy. He sounds pretty honest.'

'Well then, that's where you and I differ,' said Mr Offalbox, with narrowing eyes.

'Does this mean we're not getting our extra pudding?' asked Umer.

'The only "extra" you're getting is an hour's extra detention after school.'

'Ah, man! That ain't fair!' I said. 'It wasn't on purpose!'

'Isn't that always your excuse, Humza?' said Mr Offalbox.

'No. I've got lots of excuses. I once said a ghost broke the canteen window.'

'And did anyone believe you?'

'No.'

'And no one believes you now. So, unless you want detention every day this week, get out of this toilet immediately and take that ridiculous graffiti with you. I'll be teaching your lessons for the rest of the day. And I'm in the mood for extra homework.'

Man, Offalbox had to be the worst headmaster in the world! We used to have this nice old woman named Mrs Prume, who was pretty easy to confuse. I barely ever got caught when she was around. Then Offalbox showed up and suddenly we got detentions, extra homework, lines . . . I tell you, that ain't acceptable at primary school! How was I meant to enjoy misbehaving if I kept getting punished for it?

It was already getting dark when Umer and I got out of school. I was dragging my feet because I knew I'd be in trouble when I got home. My mum would ask me why I was late and, if I lied, she'd work it out. So I'd have to tell her the truth, and then she'd tell my dad, and then he'd threaten me with some weird punishment I've never heard of before, like a two-hour headstand or sleeping in a drawer.

Umer was looking at his phone and the screen was lighting up his face in the darkness.

'Hmm,' he said after a while. 'I'm not sure this is going to work after all.'

'What?' I asked.

He turned the phone screen to show me the footage we'd shot earlier. At least that's what I think it was. A blocky brown thing was moving near some blocky white things.

'What the hell is that, man?' I asked.

'You're the blocky brown thing,' said Umer helpfully.

'I figured that. But you can't even tell I'm handsome! Hell, you can't even tell I'm human!'

'Well, on the plus side, at least you can't tell it's a toilet either.'

'You can't tell anything! This is terrible! How old is that phone?'

'About twice as old as us,' replied Umer.

'Ah, man, this is never gonna work. Why can't you have a proper phone?'

'It's the only phone my dad will give me. Can we use yours?'

'You know I've only got a pager,' I snapped.

'What's a pager?'

I showed him the little black box my dad had given me.

'It's like a phone that only accepts text messages,' I said. 'Doctors have 'em. I think it's three times as old as we are.'

'Does it have a video camera?'

'Take a wild guess.'

'Well then, I don't know how we're going to make your music video, Humza.'

'But I've got to make it, man! How else am I gonna take over the world and leave all you suckers behind?'

'You could study hard and gain qualifications in an area you find rewarding?' suggested Umer.

'Yeah, or I could catch a leprechaun and make him grant me wishes, but both those ideas are fantasy. I've got to make this video, Umer! I've just got to!'

And that was when I saw it. We'd come to a stop outside the shops on the high street and, at first, neither of us had noticed the window display. When Umer saw me staring open-mouthed, he turned to look. Right there in the centre of the window was the most beautiful thing I had ever seen. The Matsani S3000 Home Pro Compact Video Camera. White moulded plastic with sharp black outlining. Optical zoom lens. 16-megapixel sensor. Three-inch fold-out LCD screen. And all this in a package roughly the size of a chihuahua's head. I had to have it.

'That'd do the job,' said Umer.

'That *will* do the job,' I replied.

'Really? How? It's £150.'

'Yeah, but it's marked down from £300.'

'OK, but that's still £150 more than you've got.'

'Doesn't matter,' I replied, staring at the twinkling lens in the display case. 'It's destiny, Umer. It *will* be mine . . . Oh yes . . . It *will* be mine!'

CHAPTER TWO
LITTLE BADMAN / BIG TROUBLE

' "Detention"?' shouted my dad. 'What do you mean, "detention"?'

For a second I wasn't sure if he was actually asking me what the word 'detention' meant, or whether he was just angry that I'd got in trouble again. Seriously, it could have been either. For someone who's lived here for twenty years, he's got a weird vocabulary. I swear, he still calls every type of underpants 'knickers' – even his big baggy brown Y-fronts. *Where are my knickers, woman?* It just ain't right.

'It wasn't my fault!' I replied, holding my palms up like it was a robbery. 'They made me stay after school because I saved a teacher's life.'

'Is that *really* all?' asked my mother, who stood beside him in the hallway, peering right into my soul.

'Well … I might also have been partly responsible for nearly killing her. But I swear that was mostly Umer's fault. Him and Mustafa.'

'Who is this Mustafa?' shouted my father. 'You are forbidden to spend time with him!'

'Uh … OK,' I said. 'I mean, it'll be a great sacrifice. But, if that's the full extent of my punishment, then I agree. You're a harsh but fair judge.'

'Ha!' laughed my dad. 'You think this is your punishment? Ha ha ha! Did you hear that, Nausheen? He thinks this is all the punishment I can come up with for him. Oh, no! No, no, no, no, no!'

I could tell he was starting to go off on one. That was the last thing I wanted. When my dad takes something as a personal challenge, it can only go badly wrong.

'You need discipline, boy!' he continued. 'When I was your age, I ran seventy miles to school every morning and seventy miles back. Sometimes, I was the only one who made it in, including the teachers! I had to teach myself.

And did I complain? Of course not! It is what made me the man I am today!'

Ah, man, I'd heard this one so many times I could have mouthed along with him, but I figured that would have only made things worse. So I stayed quiet. Instead I tried to guess which line he'd go for next: *How many shops do I own?* or *Look at the calluses on these hands!*

'How many shops do I own?' he asked.

'Twooo,' I said in that drawn-out way a class says good morning.

'Two. That's right! And how many bathrooms do we have in this house?'

'Threeee,' I replied.

'Three!' he barked back at me. 'Plus one in each shop – that's five bathrooms! No one in my family has ever had five bathrooms. And do you know how I have done so well?'

'Scratch cards?' I began, but he shouted over me:

'Discipline! Without discipline, you will end up like Grandpa!'

Now, just to be clear here, Grandpa ain't my grandpa – he's my uncle. Confusing, right? In fact, he ain't anyone's grandpa – he doesn't even have kids.

It's just his nickname because he's so old and tired-looking. Always has been, even when he was at school. At fifteen, he looked like a twice-divorced accountant about to get the sack. By thirty, he was bald and grey and slept twenty-seven hours a day. Nowadays I've got no idea how old he is, but if someone told me he was a thousand I'd believe them.

He looks like he's made of the stuff you empty out of a vacuum cleaner. I think maybe his only purpose in life is to be used in stories to scare little  kids into having more discipline. If it wasn't for Auntie Uzma, I reckon he'd have wasted away already.

Now, my mum had remained pretty quiet through all of this. But that doesn't mean she's any less dangerous. They just work differently. My dad's a volcano, blowing his top at the first sign of trouble. My mum, on the other hand, is a carbon monoxide leak. Silent but deadly. She'll get you and you'll barely know she was in the room.

'What do you want, Humza?' she said, when my dad had paused for breath.

'Uh, you mean like for dinner?' I asked.

'No,' she replied. 'What do you want from your life?'

Huh . . . That was unexpected.

See, that's what I'm talking about. Mums work on a whole other level to dads. While my dad's caught up trying to think of a way to throw me out of a window without getting arrested, my mum is getting straight to the important stuff.

'Well, funny you should mention it, but I want – no! – I *need* a Matsani S3000 Home Pro Compact Video Camera, so I can make the greatest rap video the world has ever seen and –'

'Video camera? What the hell are we talking about?' interrupted my father.

My mum silenced him with a stare.

'And are they expensive, these video cameras?'

'No, man! That's the best bit – only £150!' I replied.

'And do you have £150?' she asked.

'Uh, no,' I replied. I could see by the look on my dad's face that he was as confused as I was about where this was going.

'Well then, *I* am going to help you to get that money,' she continued.

'What?' my dad and I shouted at the same time.

'This boy needs discipline, not a reward!' he yelled, and again my mum silenced him with a sharp look.

'That is all I will say about it for now,' she added. 'We will discuss this later.'

I was so confused by what had just happened that I didn't even hear the doorbell ring. I just stood there next to my dad, our mouths hanging open, trying to figure out what on earth my mum was up to.

'*Hiii–eeeee!*' came the squeal as my mum opened the front door. You can always tell an auntie from their squeal. Each one's was unique. This squeal belonged to Auntie Uzma. She and my uncle, Grandpa, lived two roads away with their cat, David Chesterton.

See, their neighbour, a human named David Chesterton, had died one afternoon a few years back and his cat had just wandered next door looking for food. They didn't know the cat's name, so just started calling it 'David Chesterton's cat'. Before long it became known as David Chesterton (and occasionally just Dave). It liked curling up on Grandpa, as he spent almost exactly as much of the day asleep as David Chesterton. So that was how a cat named after an old dead white guy came to live with a big round Pakistani lady and her thousand-year-old husband. Glad you asked, huh?

Anyway, I was snapped out of my daze by a familiar pinching on my cheeks.

'Who is a beautiful fat boy?' said Auntie Uzma, squeezing the skin of my cheeks between her thumb and forefinger and wobbling them.

'Don't body-shame me, Auntie,' I said. 'Anyway, I ain't fat. I'm big boned.'

'Nonsense!' she said, smiling. 'You are too skinny. But we will fatten you up!'

And, with that, she turned to Grandpa, who was standing behind her, halfway through a big yawn, and snatched the bowl he was carrying. It was a massive pile of gulab jamun, my favourite. If you haven't had them you should. They're these sweet little balls of something. I don't know. And no one makes 'em like an auntie. Or maybe a mum if she's in a good mood – but that ain't often.

'Are these for me?' I asked, reaching for the large bowl.

'No!' she snapped, pulling it away. 'They are for your mother. She may give you one if you are good.'

'Oh, Uzma! Thank you,' said my mum. 'You didn't need to do that.'

'Nonsense. You are too skinny also,' replied

Auntie Uzma. 'You are all too skinny. And my cooking is wasted on Grandpa here. I've been trying to fatten him up for twenty years and I get nowhere. So I look after you now.'

'Oh, well, it's very kind of you,' said my mum, taking the bowl.

'You will have some now, yes?' asked my auntie.

'Now? Oh ... well, we're right in the middle of something actually,' replied my mum.

'Punishing the boy for being an idiot!' added my dad, keen to get back to it.

'Nonsense!' said Auntie Uzma, pinching one of the gulab jamun between her finger and thumb and lifting it from the bowl. 'You will have a little taste right now!'

'Really,' said my mum, 'thank you, but we've not had dinner yet and we're –'

'Just a taste!' interrupted my aunt, holding the little brown ball right up to my mum's mouth.

My mum, who was still clutching the bowl, couldn't do anything to stop her. She either had to open her mouth or have the food smushed against her teeth. So she took a bite, nodding happily.

'Mmm,' she said, before adding, 'Delicious!' when she could manage it.

I've said it before and I'll say it again: aunties are weird. You just have to go with it. And, to be fair, my parents weren't shouting at me any more, so I was pretty happy with the outcome.

'Give her another bite, Auntie,' I suggested.

'Here it comes,' said Auntie Uzma, and she pushed the gooey ball into my mum's mouth again, barely waiting for her to swallow the last piece.

My mum stared at me with quiet irritation as she chewed. I knew I was in trouble . . . Might as well enjoy it while I could.

Of course, at that time, I had no idea *how much* trouble I was in. How much trouble we were all in . . .

The next morning in the classroom, there was no sign of Miss Crumble. There was no sign of any teacher. We all sat there waiting for someone to appear, but no one came. I noticed Wendy Wang had chosen to sit further away than usual and was avoiding meeting my eye. She had on her spare glasses, which were bright yellow and too small for her head. I was just thinking that I might get up and say something to her, when the door burst open and an ogre with a moustache looked in.

'Good morning, children,' said the headmaster.

'*Gooooood mornnnning, Missstteerrr Offallllbox*,' replied the class.

'Sorry for the delay,' he continued, entering the room. 'We've been trying to find a substitute teacher for you, but have run into some problems.'

'Where's Miss Crumble?' asked Wendy Wang, looking upset.

'I'm afraid Miss Crumble's allergy to bees has proven to be rather extreme,' replied the head. 'The doctors say she'll be OK, but, due to the extent of the reaction, she's been put into what's called a medically-induced coma until the swelling goes down. It means they're keeping her asleep.'

Upon hearing this, the class all began to chatter at once.

'Quieten down, students, quieten down,' grumbled the headmaster until the noise settled. 'Now it seems, unfortunately, that there are rather a lot of teacher absences in the borough today, and there's a shortage of available substitutes. As such, we've had trouble finding someone to teach your class.'

'Can't you do it, sir?' asked Wendy Wang.

'I'm afraid I have quite enough other responsibilities to be getting on with, Wendy,' said Mr Offalbox, with a smile that made his caterpillar curl up at the edges.

'Thankfully, though,' he continued, 'we've had a volunteer from the community offer to stand in until Miss Crumble is well enough to return to work. Humza, I believe you two already know one another.'

Before I could even turn to the door, I heard the voice. The shriek . . .

'Hiii-eeeee!'

It couldn't be anyone else. Auntie Uzma. She was wearing a bright orange shalwar kameez that made her look like an enormous satsuma. Bumping the headmaster out of the way with her bottom, she dropped a large cardboard box on Miss Crumble's desk, then turned to face the class.

'Hello, children,' she said, with a beaming smile. 'I am Mrs Khan, but you can call me Auntie Uzma.'

Then she spotted me. I tried to hide behind Umer, but it was too late. She was over in a flash.

'There's my beautiful fat boy!' she said, squeezing my cheeks in her death grip.

'Gah! Get off, Auntie – I mean, miss,' I said, shaking her off.

'Class,' said the headmaster with a grin, 'Mrs Khan is Humza's aunt.'

'It's true,' said Auntie Uzma. Then she added with a giggle, 'I used to change his nappy when he was so little and fat you couldn't even see his winky!'

Oh. My. God.

The whole class burst out laughing. What was she doing to me? Was this my parents' punishment? It couldn't be. This was too cruel! This crazy old lady was going to destroy my reputation. Destroy my whole life!

'Well,' said Mr Offalbox, grinning right at me. 'I think this is going to work out swimmingly. I shall leave you to it. Just call if they give you any trouble, Mrs Khan.'

'Oh, don't you worry about me,' said Auntie Uzma. 'I know how to handle these little scamps.'

And, with that, she went to open her cardboard box. The headmaster flashed me one last grin before leaving the room. He was still punishing me; I could tell by the glint in his eye. When I turned back, Auntie Uzma was already handing out the contents of her box. Gulab jamun!

She'd made enough for the whole class and was handing them out, one to each kid. Maybe this wasn't so bad after all. Sure, she was going to ruin my life, but at least it would be tasty. When I got mine, I took a big bite straight away. *Aaahhhhhh*, man, it was good. So good. It kind of made up for the whole 'winky' story.

'It sounds like Miss Crumble's pretty ill,' said Umer between mouthfuls. 'I hope she's OK.'

'She'll be fine,' I replied. 'She's in hospital now. No one dies in hospital.'

'I guess,' said Umer, but he didn't sound convinced.

'Listen, don't worry about that. We've got more important things to think about. Like shooting the rest of the video.'

'But I thought you said my phone was worse than malaria.'

'It is, that's why we're getting that video camera.'

'How? Did you get the money?'

'No, but I'm going to. My mum said she'd help me. She just hasn't told me how yet.'

'Hmm, that sounds a bit too good to be true.'

'Nah, man, I'm sure they've just realized that every day they hold me back from being a superstar is another day they have to live in miserable poverty.'

'Yeah . . . or there's gonna be a catch.'

'A catch? What catch? Why'd there be a catch?'

'I dunno,' replied Umer. 'Mums can be tricky like that.'

Ah, man, I hate catches. What kind of catch could it be? Knowing my mum, it would be pretty bad. I was going to have to play this one carefully.

'Well,' I said, 'all I know is that, one way or another, I'm getting that camera.'

'Great,' replied Umer. 'And, after that, all that's left to do is make the track better.'

'What are you talking about, man? The track's amazing!' I snapped.

'Yeah, it's good . . . It's just . . . you know . . . not . . . *very* good.'

'Whatever. It's gonna be great when it's done. We can work on it more in our music lesson this afternoon. Mr Turnbull said he's got something to show us.'

Let me tell you about Mr Turnbull. For a guy who's, like, seventy per cent bald and wears socks with his sandals, Mr T is a sick musician. He can play pretty much every instrument there is, mix tracks on a computer, and write a beat so tight it makes my dad look generous. He ain't like the rest of the teachers. He's a pretty cool guy. That's why he's helping us with the track. When things work out, maybe I'll make him my producer and rescue him from this place. A lot of big stars do charity work. That could be mine.

'Now, children,' said Auntie Uzma, 'what have you been studying this wee–'

But she never finished the sentence, because that was when we heard the crash. Something heavy in a nearby room had fallen over with a *boom!* It was followed immediately by a terrible scream.

At the time I couldn't be a hundred per cent sure, but, if I had to guess, I'd have said it sounded exactly like a librarian being squashed by a bookshelf . . .

CHAPTER THREE
PUNISHMENT TIME

We were out at lunch break when the ambulance men finally carried the librarian through on a stretcher.

'Poor Mrs Finigan,' said Umer, watching the old lady being loaded into the back of the ambulance. 'Crushed by the books she loved.'

'Tell me about it,' I replied. 'If she'd been stood in the early readers section, maybe she'd be OK. But some of those later Harry Potter books are massive. It's a miracle she wasn't killed. I told you reading was dangerous.'

'Two teachers in two days,' said Umer. 'That's pretty bad luck.'

'Well, Finigan ain't really a teacher, so it probably only counts as a half. That ain't too bad.'

'I always liked her,' said Umer, frowning.

'I hope she's OK.'

You know, whatever his failings (and there's loads of 'em), you've got to give it to Umer – he's a good egg.

'Come on,' I said, putting my arm round his shoulder. 'Let's go get some lunch.'

Five minutes later we were queuing up in the canteen. It smelled healthy, in the worst way. That over-boiled vegetable stink – like a wet dog in a hot car, or a fart in a sauna, or my dad's pants in the microwave (seriously, that's a thing that happens at my house). Anyway, you get the idea. Nasty.

'Ah, man, I hope it's not mystery stew,' I said, trying to stand on tiptoes to see what was being served. 'The only mystery is how long it'll take to throw up afterwards.'

'I don't mind it,' said Umer. 'I just pretend I'm eating something I like that's been put through a blender.'

'Does it taste better that way?'

'A bit,' replied Umer. 'I definitely gag less.'

At that point, Wendy Wang walked by, holding her tray.

'What is it, Wendy?' I asked, leaning over to see.

'More delicious mystery stew,' she said, inhaling

the aroma of her stew until it fogged up her glasses.

'Ah, man. You can't *actually* like it, can you?' I asked.

'What do you mean?' replied Wendy. 'It's got a balanced mix of nutrients and flavours. It's a perfect-sized helping. And it goes great with a nice glass of cool tap water.'

'Really? That's your serving suggestion, tap water? Man, this lunch is more depressing than when my dog died.'

'What did he die of?' asked Umer.

'Depression,' I replied, and stepped up to the front of the queue.

'Rice or potatoes?' said Moira, the dinner lady with the long face.

'Which is worse today?' I asked.

She looked at me for a moment to work out if I was being rude or not. She seemed to decide it was a fair question.

'The rice,' she said, scratching her hairy chin. 'It's burnt.'

'Excellent. One portion of potatoes, please,' I replied.

She plonked the mushy white potatoes on top of my steaming stew and turned to serve Umer.

We ate as quickly as you can eat something that looks like it came out of a blocked drain, then we ran off to the best lesson of the week: music with Mr Turnbull.

'Shouldn't you boys still be at lunch?' asked Mr Turnbull, who was busy placing a recorder on every seat in the music room.

'We wanted to get started on the track,' I said, opening his laptop. 'What's the password for this?'

'Hang on, hang on,' he said, closing the laptop. 'I'm pleased to see how enthusiastic you are about it all, Humza, but we're going to be doing some work on the recorders today.'

'Recorders?' I spluttered. 'Why would we do that? We've got real music to make.'

'We can make music on the recorders,' he replied.

'That ain't music! Have you heard the noise this class makes when they get a hold of those things? It's like someone beating a donkey with a dolphin!'

'That's a very vivid image, Humza,' he said. 'I don't think anyone's ever described my lesson like that before.'

'Exactly! I'm a lyrical master,' I said, opening his laptop again. 'We've got to get this track mixed so

I can share my gift with the world.'

'Look,' said Mr Turnbull, closing the laptop again before putting it out of reach on a shelf. 'If you can get through the assignment I've set for you, then, once the rest of the class are working on their compositions, we can have a look at your track. Deal?'

'Hmm,' I said, thinking his offer through. 'I don't think Eminem has to work under these conditions, but I guess I'm gonna have to live with it. Deal.'

Umer and I took a seat and started mucking about with the recorders until the rest of the class came in.

What followed was an hour of the worst noise you can get out of thirty-five healthy kids. Seriously, Mr Turnbull must meditate or something because any normal person would go nuts if he had to do this even twice in a lifetime.

'OK, boys,' said Mr Turnbull. 'Come and grab a seat at my desk.'

'Finally!' I said. 'There's only ten minutes left!'

'I've got something good to show you. Ten minutes is all we need.'

Umer and I dragged our seats over to Mr Turnbull's desk while the rest of the class worked on permanently damaging their hearing. Mr Turnbull opened up his laptop and the audio mixing software he used. I saw the file name at the top: 'Badman Demo Rough'. The track wasn't much to speak of yet, just a rough recording of some of my rap lyrics (though they'd need to be updated, as I'd tightened them up a lot since then). And below that were some beats that Mr Turnbull had been experimenting with.

'Now, I've had a little tinker with it since you heard it last. Made a few improvements. Have a listen,' he said, handing us each a pair of headphones.

As he hit PLAY, all the colourful boxes along

the timeline began to glide to the left. Each little rectangle – red, blue, green, yellow – represented a bit of the track. Maybe it was a drumbeat, maybe it was a vocal, but as they slid past the playhead we could hear them kick in through the headphones.

'DAMN!' I said, too loudly, because I couldn't hear myself. 'THIS IS SOUNDING GOOD!'

Mr Turnbull smiled and made a 'shh!' sign. Whatever the beat was that Mr T had come up with, it was incredible. And the bass . . . I couldn't even figure out what I was hearing – it was like an explosion going backwards. Then my vocal kicked in. *Hmm*, I thought, *I can do better than that*. I definitely had a better performance in me. And my new lyrics were ten times as good – though there were still a few tight rhymes in this version:

'My rhymes are so sick, other MCs sicken.
Best not speak when I'm eating fried chicken.
But my local KFC ain't a halal one.
So I gotta drive to Taply with my dad and mum.'

The playhead skimmed over the last of the coloured blocks and the track came to an end. Umer and I grinned at each other.

'Sir, that was amazing!' I said, taking off my headphones.

'It's incredible!' said Umer.

'Thought you'd like that,' Mr Turnbull said with a smile. 'It's been fun to play with. I don't get to do enough of that any more.'

'Is that cos you gave up on your dreams and became a teacher?' I asked him.

'Yeah, something like that,' he said, laughing, and he closed the laptop. 'Now, come on – we'd better start packing up.'

'Aw, sir, can't we do some more work on it?' I begged. 'I've got to redo my vocals. They're well out of date.'

'Not today, boys. Come and see me in the week and we'll find some time.'

Man, I couldn't get that beat out of my head for the rest of the day. Mr T had outdone himself. Imagine if every teacher was like him . . . School would actually be good!

The afternoon went pretty quick after that. I was in such a good mood I didn't even mind Auntie Uzma being weird. Well, I didn't mind it *that* much. She pinched my cheeks a lot and told a story about how I wore a dress for a month when I was three, but I was too busy thinking about the track to let it get me down.

When the bell went at 3 p.m., I was out of my seat and flying down the stairs before you could say, *Humza, come back! I haven't dismissed the class yet!* I just wanted to get to that shop again and stare at that video camera for at least an hour. Maybe I'd ask them if I could touch it.

But as I got to the main doors I stopped dead in my tracks. There in front of me was a sight no boy ever wants to see: Dad talking to the headmaster. Uh-oh. I'd been so happy about the track I'd totally forgotten about my punishment. But I knew my dad hadn't. Dads never forget. I had to get out of there fast.

It looked like they hadn't seen me yet, so I turned on my heel and ran back the other way. If I was quick, I could get out the side exit and take the long route round. Sometimes putting off a punishment is the best option available.

'Where are you going?' said Umer as I sprinted past him.

'Danger that way! Meet me at the shop,' I said and disappeared round the corner. As I ran out the back door, I felt pretty sure I was home free. Then I spotted her, standing in the side gateway, staring straight at me . . .

'Oh, hi, Mum,' I said, skidding to a halt. 'Fancy seeing you here.'

'You and I need to have a little chat,' she said, walking slowly towards me.

'Uh . . . I'm meant to meet Umer in a minute. Can it wait until later? Maybe February?'

'Do you want that camera or not?' asked my mum.

She had me there.

'All right,' I said, folding my arms. 'I think we both know I need that camera. So what's the catch?'

'No catch. You're just going to have to work for it.'

'Work for it? But I've already got a full-time job. I go to school!'

'And you finish school at 3 p.m. So I've arranged a job for you in the afternoons.'

'Child labour's illegal! This ain't Victorian times.'

'After-school jobs are fine. And if you can make a go of this one for a whole month, then I will make a contribution towards this camera of yours.'

'Really? How much?'

'Say . . . half?'

Hmm, it was actually a pretty good deal. But it all came down to one thing:

'What am I gonna be doing?' I asked.

'Every day, for two hours, you will be helping out with your uncle, Grandpa.'

'Grandpa? Why? What help does he need? All he does is sleep!'

'Now that your auntie is going to be busy at the school, someone has to look after Grandpa.'

'Can't he look after himself?'

'I think we both know the answer to that.'

'Aw, man, this is totally unfair! I don't want to spend two hours a day with Grandpa. He smells like mothballs and daal.'

'I don't see that you have many options. Not if you ever want to own this video camera of yours.'

I could see she was right. Damn. I hate it when mums are right. They get this little glint of power in their eyes, like a cat messing with its prey. The only way I could win this was to play by her rules, so that at least eventually she'd have to cough up her half of the money.

'Fine. It's a deal,' I said. 'But I ain't changing his nappy. No camera in the world is worth that much.'

Mum just smiled. 'Come on,' she said. 'Let's go home.'

'What about Dad?' I asked.

'What do you mean?'

'He's here. Inside. Isn't he with you?'

'Your father's in the school? I don't know anything about that. What was he doing?'

'Talking to the headmaster.'

'Hmm, I wonder what that's about,' she said, looking puzzled. Suddenly I had that sinking feeling again. But it didn't take long to find out why he was there.

'Ah, there you are!' came a surprisingly cheerful version of my dad's voice.

I turned round to see him come bowling out of the school with a dangerous smile on his face.

'What are you doing here?' asked my mum.

'What am *I* doing here? What are *you* doing here?' replied my dad. Then he continued, before she could even answer, 'I am here to make punishment for the boy!'

'Ah, man! Isn't one punishment enough? I didn't even do anything!' I said, but no one was listening.

'The boy needs discipline,' continued my father. 'When I was his age, I had so much discipline I could hold my breath for one hour, not eat for a month and sleep for only six minutes a night. Pakistan Ministry of Defence tried to recruit me as a spy.'

'Yeah, right,' I said, not believing a word of it. 'But instead you chose to come here and open a shop, yeah?'

'Of course!' he replied. 'Still the best decision I ever made. I can guarantee you, whatever fool took that spy job does not own half as many toilets as me!'

My mum rolled her eyes.

'Now,' he continued, 'I have discussed it with your headmaster and he has agreed to let you join the cricket team.'

'Cricket? I don't know how to play cricket!'

'Yes you do,' replied my dad. 'It is in your genes. Like heart disease from your mother's side.'

Mum frowned at him but let him go on with his rant.

'He has let you join on one condition: I have arranged for the team to be coached by one of Pakistan's most celebrated cricket captains –'

'Oh no . . .' I said – I could see where this was going.

'Me,' he added, with a satisfied smile.

'You?' replied my mum. 'You are one of Pakistan's most celebrated cricket captains?'

'Of course I am, woman!' said my dad. 'I have won so many trophies I had to leave them behind in a warehouse in Karachi!'

Ah, man, he's done this my whole life. Tells these stories about Pakistan and the things he did there. When you're little you just believe them all, even though they're ridiculous. I only realized last year that he probably never punched a bear so hard that it forgot it was a bear and let him raise it as a dog. But when you're five that seems like a pretty cool thing for your dad to have done. These days it's a nightmare.

'Look,' I said, 'I can't do it, Abu-jee.' (Abu-jee just means 'Dad', but it's what I call him when I'm trying to get on his good side.) 'Mum's already punished me with an after-school job, so I won't be around to go to practice.'

'What?' he shouted. 'Nonsense! You cannot do an after-school job; you have cricket practice!'

'Firstly, I'm not punishing you,' said my mother. 'I'm offering you an opportunity to work for what you want. Though I agree with your father: you do lack discipline. Secondly, there's no reason why you can't do both. How many nights a week will he practise?'

'Eight!' shouted my father.

'Mohammed . . .' she said with a hint of steel in her voice.

'Fine, five at least,' replied my dad. 'Any less is impossible!'

'The other boys will not be able to do five. I think three will be adequate.'

'*Three?*' shouted my dad. 'How will he improve, with only three nights' practice a week?'

'Doesn't he have one of the greatest coaches Pakistan has ever known?' asked my mother.

'This is true,' agreed my father. 'Perhaps three will be enough.'

'Good,' said my mother. 'And three days a week, you will work for two hours helping Grandpa. Sundays will be your own.'

'Helping Grandpa?' said my dad. 'Ha! I like this punishment after all!'

'It's not a punishment,' said my mum. 'It's a job. One month gets you halfway to this video camera of yours,' she reminded me.

'Ah!' said my dad, nodding his head. 'Incentive.

Very clever. I like this! Tell you what, if you become a valued member of the cricket team, then I shall pay for other half.'

Wow! That was unlike him. I knew he loved cricket, but to part with money? He must really care about this. He didn't even ask how much.

'What if I can't do it?' I said.

'Then you will not get your camera,' replied my mum.

'And you will be sent to live in Pakistan until you are thirty-five,' added my dad.

'What?' I shouted.

'If you do not start winning tournaments, you will be going to live with Uncle Farooq in Karachi until your thirty-fifth birthday. Perhaps a proper Pakistani upbringing will give you the discipline you need.'

'Mohammed!' said my mother, rolling her eyes.

'Nausheen!' snapped my father. 'I have spoken!'

Mum just shook her head.

What had just happened? My head was spinning. Babysitting Grandpa, winning cricket tournaments? Were they mad? Had they even met me? I couldn't do those things! Not well, anyway. I was just about to protest, when the doors behind me opened and a zombie came barging out. Actually, it was Mrs Aguda, the nursery teacher, but there was something wrong with her.

'*Guuhhhh*,' she groaned. 'Get out of my way!'

There were red spots all over her face, all over her arms and her legs. She was staggering, scratching at her skin, moaning. We all jumped out of the way and let her stumble past. She wandered out the gate and disappeared round the corner.

'What on earth was that?' said my mother.

We didn't know it at the time, but the answer would turn out to be adult chicken pox – a real nasty case. The other thing, which we couldn't have known, was that, after rushing out of the school gates that afternoon, Mrs Aguda was about to vanish into thin air.

And she wouldn't be the only one . . .

CHAPTER FOUR
GRANDPA'S GREATEST TRICK

Have you ever seen one of those vampire movies, when they enter the crypt or the castle or whatever, and there's dust in the air and not much light and you know there's a monster in there but you don't know where?

That's exactly what it felt like when we opened the door of Grandpa's house a few days later. Auntie Uzma was still at school, doing whatever teachers do after the bell goes, so Mum had let us in with her spare key. There was no sign of Grandpa ...

I still didn't even know what I was doing there. Grandpa-sitting? Sure, he eats mushy food, wears a nappy at night and sleeps most of the day – but he ain't a baby. *I'm* the kid here. *He* should be looking after *me*.

'Can we leave?' I said, as we stood in the

doorway looking in. 'This place smells weird. It's like someone opened a curry house in a hospital.'

'Of course you can leave,' replied Mum, '. . . in two hours.'

'Ah, man! If you just buy the camera for me now, I can make at least seven million quid by the end of the week and pay you straight back. That way neither of us have to spend time with an old man.'

'This old man is your uncle and you are lucky to be able to take care of him. All my uncles are back home in Rawalpindi. I wish *I* could spend a day with *them*.'

'Well how about we swap? I'll go home and watch bad soap operas and you can stay here with Skeletor.'

She grabbed me by the collar before I could get away and yanked me back into the house. The door slammed behind us. We were alone in the dark. Something moved in the shadows . . .

'Grandpa?' said Mum.

'*Purr-rr*,' replied David Chesterton, stepping into the hall. He tilted his head and stared at us. We were obviously not who he was expecting.

'Hello, David Chesterton,' said Mum.

'Wa-gwan, David Chesterton?' I added, bending down to give him a little fist bump.

I'd taught him it a few months back, using bits of chicken as a reward. It only took five hours.

'*Purr-rrp, roo-ouuw*,' replied David Chesterton, tapping my fist with his paw.

I don't usually like cats, but David Chesterton was OK. He had a great big fuzzy face and looked like a professor or a wizard or something. He was a mix of swirly browns, light and dark, and had a tail like a feather duster. His hair was so long and so thick you'd find it on you for days after you left. But, like I say, he was a pretty cool cat, so I didn't hold it against him.

'You seen Grandpa, boy?' I asked him.

David Chesterton turned and looked behind him into the darkness. There was a gentle snoring coming from the living room.

'Something tells me he's in his usual spot,' said Mum.

We found him on the living-room sofa with one of my auntie's magazines draped over his face. The front cover had a pretty serious-looking portrait of the Queen on it. She looked like the photographer had just let one off and she wasn't too impressed. The best bit though was that the magazine had slipped perfectly over Grandpa's face, like a mask – so it looked like there was a wide-awake, slightly irritable Queen chilling out on Auntie Uzma's sofa. You ain't really seen the Queen until you've seen her with big yellow toenails and a curry-stained cardigan. Man, I wished I had a smartphone right then.

'Grandpa,' said Mum, gently touching his shoulder. 'Humza's here to look after you.'

'Unless you'd rather just sleep?' I added quickly. 'In which case, we're happy to leave.'

The Queen began to stretch and sit up. As she did, the magazine slipped down and revealed a bleary-eyed Grandpa underneath.

'All right, Uncle?' I said.

'Hello, boy,' said Grandpa with a cheeky smile. His teeth were all over the place: loads missing, all different yellows and browns, and seriously long. They were like funny little tombstones, wonky and exposed, all the way down to his elephant-grey gums. But for some reason it made for a great smile. Under all the wrinkles and cobwebs, there was still a kid in there somewhere.

'Now, Uzma's going to be back in a few hours,' said Mum in that louder-than-normal voice she used for Grandpa and other old-looking people. 'Humza's going to stay here and take care of you.'

'Why?' asked Grandpa, scratching his head.

'Exactly!' I said. 'Grandpa gets it. He doesn't need me here. We could save everyone a lot of time and effort if you just paid me the money anyway and let Grandpa go back to sleep.'

'They pay you to come?' asked Grandpa, looking puzzled.

'Damn right,' I said. 'My time is valuable.'

Grandpa's smile had gone now. His eyebrows seemed to sink a little. 'Oh,' was all he said.

A few minutes later Mum let herself out, leaving me all alone with Grandpa. As the door clicked shut it struck me that I couldn't remember a time I'd ever hung out with him by himself. Maybe for, like, five minutes while Auntie Uzma went to find a toilet in the shopping centre, but not properly, not like this.

I had a vague memory of sitting on his knee as a kid while he made up stories. But even then Mum or some auntie was always hanging about nearby. It felt pretty weird to be sitting here, just the two of us. I mean, what the hell did *we* have to talk about?

'Uh ... so ... what do we do now?' I asked.

Grandpa gave a small shrug. I could tell he was as thrown by this as I was.

'You want a nap?' suggested Grandpa.

'Uh, not really,' I replied. 'It's half past three in the afternoon.'

'Oh,' he said with a little smile, like this was new information to him.

We sat there quietly again. David Chesterton licked his paw and rubbed it on his head. That always struck me as a pretty stupid way to get clean: lick the thing you walk around on, rub it somewhere dirty, then lick it again. I think I'd rather just smell.

'You like magic tricks?' asked Grandpa out of the blue.

'Huh?' I replied.

It was the last thing I'd expected him to say. Well, I guess if he had said, *I ate all the fridge magnets*, or, *The dishwasher has human feet*, I might have expected that a bit less. But still . . . magic. It wasn't exactly what you expect from Grandpa (even though he *does* kinda look like a Pakistani Dumbledore).

'Come, come, come,' he said, heaving himself off the sofa.

Man, what a noise. Have you ever cracked your knuckles? Now imagine that sound if your *whole body* was made out of knuckles – knuckles for knees, knuckles for elbows, knuckles for knuckles . . . That's what it sounded like when Grandpa pulled himself up. Bones and muscles and tendons all popping and stretching at the same time as they struggled to stop Grandpa falling to pieces right there in the lounge.

I followed him up the stairs – which took ages, as he was a billion years old. David Chesterton tagged along too, probably because it was the most action he'd seen in months. When we got to the landing Grandpa reached for the hatch that led into the loft. His spine stretching out sounded like someone popping bubble wrap.

Standing on his tiptoes, he managed to hook a bony finger into the pulley that hung from the little trapdoor. He gave it a yank and the hatch fell open, revealing a rickety-looking ladder.

'You're not gonna climb that, are you, Uncle?' I asked him. 'Cos if that's the magic trick, I don't wanna see it.'

'Come, come, come,' was all he'd say, and up he climbed into the loft, wobbling all over the place on the shaky old ladder.

David Chesterton and I looked at each other.

'If he dies while I'm babysitting, do you reckon they'll still let me have the camera?' I said.

'Mew,' replied David Chesterton.

'Nope . . . me neither . . .'

Like Grandpa, the loft was dark, cobwebby and weird-smelling.

The dim light bulb flickered a bit as I looked around the place. Stacked all over were big cardboard boxes, marked 'Uzma' or 'Tariq'.

'Who's Tariq?' I asked.

Grandpa smiled his gummy grin and pointed a knobbly finger at his chest.

'Oh yeah,' I said. 'I forgot you had a proper name, Uncle Tariq. So what are we doing up here? Where's the magic at?'

Grandpa reached up and took one of the 'Tariq' boxes down from the stack, placing it on the ground between the three of us. David Chesterton was definitely interested now. No cat in the world can resist an empty cardboard box. Opening it up, Grandpa reached in and removed an intricately carved wooden chest. It looked like it might have been as old as Grandpa himself.

'When I was your age,' he said, 'I loved only magic tricks. I went to see the magicians in the markets; men who can float upon a length of rope or charm a cobra. I watched them every day, read of them in books. I had to know all their tricks, all their secrets.'

As he spoke, Grandpa placed the wooden chest down on the floorboards between us. David Chesterton didn't waste any time in taking its place inside the cardboard box. He sat with his head poking out the top, watching us intently. Grandpa flipped open the rusty iron catch, which held the box shut. The ancient hinges groaned as he raised the lid.

Inside, was an explosion of colour. Too much to take in at once, it seemed almost to glow in the darkness of the attic.

'Whoa!' was all I could manage.

There were coins and cards and slips of silk. There were shiny cups and fuzzy red balls. There were magic wands, lengths of rope and a chain of sparkling silver rings. It was much better and much messier than any of those magic kits you can get at the shops. I didn't know where to start.

'What is it all?' I asked him.

'Oh, lots and lots. Many different things,' he replied, that grin returning to his face.

'OK, well, what's your favourite one?'

'Ah,' he replied. 'The trick I love best is still my first. The first I ever learned.'

He scooped out a small grubby coin from the bottom of the chest and examined it between his knobbly fingers. He moved it about between his fingertips and his thumbs like he was trying to remember how it felt. His fingers slid lightly across the coin. The coin slid smoothly between his fingers. It was weird, but somehow they didn't seem like Grandpa's fingers at all. They were so quick. So nimble. The little copper piece began to slip across his knuckles and between each finger, as though walking by itself.

'How'd you do that?' I asked him. 'How'd you

make it walk like that?'

'Just practice. You can do it too,' he said, closing the coin in his other hand and holding his fist out towards me. 'But that is not the trick.'

'What is then?' I asked, holding out my own hand to accept the coin.

'This,' he replied, pointing to his outstretched fist.

He blew gently upon his fingers; then, one by one, he peeled them open to reveal an empty palm. The coin had vanished.

'Whoa!' I gasped. 'Where'd it go?'

'David Chesterton has it,' he replied.

We both looked over towards where David Chesterton was sitting, his face poking out of the box. Right on the top of his head was the little coin.

'How did you . . . ?' I began.

'Magic, of course,' said Grandpa with a toothy grin.

'Grandpa!'

'OK, OK,' he said, laughing. 'The secret of all good sleight of hand is misdirection.'

'What's "misdirection"?'

'To make people see one thing, so they fail to see another.'

'Can you teach me?' I asked, taking the coin from David Chesterton's head.

'Of course,' said Grandpa. 'But you must do two things.'

'No problem. What?'

'The first is to practise. Practise, practise, practise. Never show a trick you have not mastered.'

'All right. What's the second?'

'The trick is your secret. You must protect it. Magic trick is only magic if audience believes. Only share very rarely – like I share with you now. And when you master this I teach you a new trick, agreed?'

'Yeah, agreed,' I said.

'Good. Then, watch,' he said with a grin, lifting out a second copper coin to demonstrate with. 'The secret of the disappearing coin . . .'

For the next ten minutes Grandpa showed me exactly how to perform the disappearing coin trick. (And if you want to learn it yourself, I've done a drawing at the end to help you – but don't forget Grandpa's two rules!)

I sat there practising and practising, over and over again. The trick was in making it look natural when you hid the coin from the audience.

And it wasn't easy. I don't know how long I sat there performing the trick for David Chesterton in his box, but I hadn't even noticed the snoring.

'So why's it your favourite trick then?' I asked, but there was no answer.

I looked up to see Grandpa leaning back on a pile of boxes, fast asleep and snoring away. His fingers were twitching a little, like he was having a dream. I smiled. Maybe this wouldn't be so bad after all. I mean, I was gonna get paid to hang out with Grandpa and learn magic. That was a pretty good result.

I was just about to go back to practising when I heard the door close downstairs.

'*Hiii-eeeee!*' came the shriek from below.

I was ready to shout back, but I suddenly realized it might just give Grandpa a heart attack.

'Grandpa,' I said quietly, putting my hand on his shoulder. 'Uncle, wake up. Auntie Uzma's home.'

Grandpa opened his eyes and looked about. For a moment he seemed a bit surprised to find that he was in the loft. Then he smiled.

'Have you been practising?' he asked.

'Yeah,' I replied. 'For ages. I'm getting good.'

'Excellent,' he said, and pulled himself up with

the usual cracks and creaks. 'Let's go down now. Before we get caught,' he added with a toothy grin.

'Yeah, I bet Auntie doesn't like seeing you up that ladder.'

'Yes, but old Grandpa is younger than he looks,' he said with a wink.

We had just closed the hatch when Auntie Uzma appeared at the top of the stairs.

'Ah, there you are,' she said. 'What have you two been up to?'

Before anyone could reply, David Chesterton let out a loud hiss. His fur was standing up on end and he looked like he was ready for a fight. He was staring right at Auntie Uzma. But instead of attacking her, as I thought he might, he just turned and ran into the spare bedroom, disappearing under the bed.

'What was that about?' I asked.

'He is probably just hungry,' said Auntie Uzma, shaking her head. 'Grandpa also is grumpy when he is hungry. They both need fattening up!'

'I don't know, Auntie. He's a pretty fat cat already,' I replied. 'If anything, he could stand to lose a few.'

'Nonsense!' said Auntie Uzma. 'You all need

fattening up! Now come downstairs and let us eat.'

'Actually, I think I'm meant to be eating at home.'

'You can do both,' she said with a matter-of-fact nod.

'Uh, yeah, but I probably shouldn't. My mum'll get annoyed.'

'Oh, don't you worry about her. What about a nice pudding before you go? I still have gulab jamun left over from school?'

'Hmm . . . ' I replied. 'I guess one couldn't hurt.'

'Exactly!' said Auntie Uzma. 'And two will be even better!'

Three gulab jamuns later I arrived home, licking sugary syrup off my fingers. As I opened the door the aroma of butter chicken hit me like a delicious brick in the face.

'Dinner's ready!' called my mum.

Despite me already being full to the brim with sugary goodness dinner actually smelled pretty great. I tell you, life can be tough sometimes but it looked like I was just going to have to eat more delicious food.

'How was it with Grandpa?' asked Mum as

I walked into the kitchen.

'Good actually,' I replied, still feeling a bit surprised by it all. 'Grandpa's pretty cool – you know – for an old guy.'

'I'm pleased to hear it,' said Mum, with a smile. 'Now, please, lay the table,' she added, holding a fistful of cutlery out towards me.

'Uh-oh, no way!' I said, whipping my hands away. 'I've clocked out. No more chores for me. This is Humza time.'

'Oh, really? And do you still like pocket money?'

'Uh, yeah . . .'

'Then normal chores apply,' she added, and she thrust the cutlery into my hands.

'Ah, man . . .' I muttered, and walked off to lay the table.

You know, I don't think my parents ever worked as hard as me. Sure, they grew up in rural Pakistan and had to walk a hundred miles to get water every day, but they never did SATs or had to unload a dishwasher. Life for modern kids is stressful.

I was just laying out the last of the forks when I heard a noise from behind me.

'BEHOLD!' came a booming, exaggerated voice, like some Bollywood villain.

I turned round to see a potbellied figure dressed in dazzling white from head to toe.

'Damn, Dad! What are you wearing?' I asked, squinting at the sight of him.

'My old cricket whites,' he said, clearly excited. 'They still fit perfectly!'

'Perfectly' was a bit of a stretch. They were tight like cling film and bulging at the seams. Little bits of Dad-coloured flesh could be seen forcing their way out between the buttons and over the belt.

'You ain't gonna wear that out of the house, are you?' I asked him.

'Of course I am!' he snapped. 'I have to look the part when I teach you and your boyfriends to play cricket tomorrow!'

'Tomorrow?' I yelled, even more worried about how quickly this was all happening than I was about Dad's confusion over the word 'boyfriends'.

'That's right!' he said, grinning like a madman. 'At exactly fifteen hundred hours tomorrow, your father will once again make cricketing history.'

Before I could reply, Dad hurled a plastic bag full of clothes at me.

'And remember your kit, or you will play in your knickers!'

CHAPTER FIVE
COACH KHAN

'Right!' shouted my dad, rubbing the cricket ball against a red patch on his tight white trousers. 'Today is the day everything changes! Today is the day you stop being babies and you become men!'

'I'm a girl,' replied Roberta Glott, the best girl on the cricket team – but my dad just ignored her.

I knew this would suck, but with my dad you can never tell quite how bad it's gonna be. It turns out he was just getting started.

'You,' he said, pointing a finger at Jamal Jones, 'what is your name?'

'Jamal,' replied Jamal.

'Good. Who is the greatest cricketer in history, Jamal?'

'Brian Lara,' said Jamal, sounding confident.

'Wrong. The answer is me,' said my dad

with a big smile, before turning to Imran Yusuf. 'You, moustache, what was the best cricket match ever played?'

'Uh . . . India versus Pakistan, 1986?' replied Imran.

'Ha, no! It was Manora Beach, 1974. My cousins Rabi, Ali and Jad versus the men from the tyre factory. I scored 310 runs, humiliating the staff at Siddiki Tyres for generations to come!'

The team began to mutter to one another about what was going on here. I put my head in my hands and prayed for it all to end.

'You, Humza!' he shouted, pointing the bat at me. 'What is the secret to great cricket?'

'What? I don't know! I don't even know why I'm here!' I replied.

'Shut up, boy. Answer the question! What is the secret to great cricket?'

While I might not have known anything about cricket, I *did* know my dad. I realized exactly what he was going for. I sighed.

'. . . A great coach,' I said, sounding as miserable as I felt.

'YES! A great coach is the secret to great cricket. With a great coach you can achieve anything!

And you kids have the greatest coach that Pakistan, and therefore the world, has ever known!'

The team looked at each other, confused.

'It seems obvious to me that only one of you has the potential to be a suitable captain for this team. My son, Humza!'

'What?' I shouted.

'No way!' said a voice from behind.

'He can't be captain!' came another.

'We've got a captain,' said a third.

'Quiet now!' shouted my father. 'I am the coach, so I will pick the captain.'

'But, Mr Khan, I'm already captain,' said Jamal. 'I've been captain for two years. I play every day! I even play for county juniors – and I'm a year too young.'

'You play for county team?' said my dad, looking interested. 'Then you will ask them for a place for my Humza.'

'I don't think they're looking for someone like Humza right now,' replied Jamal.

'Once he captains this team to a win at the All Schools Tournament, then we will see!'

Oh, man . . . if babysitting Grandpa had turned out better than I thought, this had turned out a hundred times worse. I just wanted to disappear. To change school. To move to Australia. Anything to not be here right now. The whole team was looking at me like this was my fault. I'd be lucky to make it through a week like this, let alone a whole season.

We started with batting practice. But this wasn't normal batting practice. See, Dad had put his own weird little twist on everything. Of course he had. So, instead of hitting normal balls, we'd be hitting grapes. Yup, grapes.

'If you can master hitting a tiny little grape, then you will never miss a great big cricket ball!' he declared, popping a grape in his mouth.

He then spent the next half hour throwing grapes at us while we attempted to hit them.

'This is stupid,' said Jamal, walking back to the group after he'd been up to bat grapes at my dad. 'I can already hit a cricket ball. I don't need to hit grapes.'

'Tell me about it, man,' I said, doing my best to laugh it off. 'Who practises with grapes, right?'

Jamal just stared at me like I was something a dog had thrown up. The rest of the team did the same.

'Am I right, guys? Grapes? What's that about?' I said, my voice starting to crack a little.

'He's *your* dad,' replied Jamal. 'Fix it.'

They all turned their backs on me and began muttering among themselves.

Cricket – what a great way to make new friends! I couldn't wait for this to be over. At least practice couldn't get any stupider than grapes.

Could it?

After grape practice, it was time to improve our stamina. And what better way to train than digging holes? Yup, Dad had brought a spade for everyone and set us the task of digging holes in the school field.

'When I was your age,' he yelled, 'I dug three dozen holes a day. Once I dug a hole so deep there was no gravity at the bottom!'

'What?' said Asif Amir. 'What's he on about?'

'Just don't listen to it,' I replied. 'I think he might have a condition. He just can't stop making this stuff up.'

'Digging holes is why I have such strong arms!' continued Dad. 'Even to this day I can lift an adult cow.'

'He has *literally* never done that,' I whispered to Asif.

'Now, do not stop digging until your hole is at least your own height!' shouted my dad.

'Aw, what?' said Yusuf Shah, who'd just gone through a freaky growth spurt and was already nearly six feet tall. 'I can't dig no six-foot hole!'

'Not with that attitude!' replied my dad, and he threw a grape at him.

An hour later we were all standing in holes two feet deep, having hit an impenetrable layer of rock.

'Dad, man!' I called from my hole. 'You'd need dynamite to get through this. Can we stop?'

'Yeah, Mr Khan,' said Jamal. 'Can't we play some cricket now? Or just go home?'

'Ha!' laughed my dad. 'You cannot do either of those things. You are not ready.'

'I'm *definitely* ready to go home,' I said.

'Shut up, boy!' said my dad. 'It is time for catching practice.'

At which point he turned on a hose attached to one wall of the school and began to spray us with water.

'Aargh! What you doing, man?' I shouted at him, desperately trying to get out of the way.

The rest of the team were yelling too. 'Turn it off!' 'What's wrong with you?' 'This is abuse!'

But Dad just shouted over them. 'When I was your age,' he yelled, 'I could pick out a raindrop from a mile up in the sky and catch it before it touched the ground!'

'No you couldn't!' shouted one of the boys from behind me, but Dad ignored him.

'When I spray the hose at you,' continued Dad, 'select a droplet, keep your eye on it and snatch it from the sky. Once you can master this technique, you will be able to catch any ball you set your sights on.'

I don't think anyone even bothered trying this one. They all just ran about like headless chickens, trying to avoid getting sprayed by the old lunatic. We were all drenched to the bone within five minutes. It continued for another half hour . . .

Finally, when that ordeal was over, we were allowed to go home. The team marched towards the gates in silence. All you could hear was the squelching of our shoes.

'Uh, good practice, team . . .' I said with an awkward smile.

Every single one of them stared at me with hate in their eyes.

'Ah, come on, guys!' I said. 'It ain't my fault. I don't want to be here just as much as you don't want me here. And think about it – you only have to see him three times a week. I have to live with him!'

'This is on you, Humza,' said Jamal, prodding me in the chest. 'Either you get rid of him, or we get rid of you.'

'From the team?' I said, hopefully.

'From the planet,' he growled.

They walked off, leaving me alone at the school gates. For a moment, all I could hear was the water dripping from my clothes and the fading squelch of their shoes. Then, from round the corner, there came a screech of tyres as Dad pulled up in our car. He looked me up and down briefly, then shook his head.

'You are too wet to get in the car,' he announced. 'You will walk home.'

And with that he drove off.

It was now official. I hated cricket.

The next day at school I tried to keep my head down. We had assembly first thing, and I spotted Jamal Jones and some other kids from the team sitting together on the far side of the hall. I didn't even want to meet their eyes. I just stared at the coin in my hand as I practised Grandpa's magic trick. I was working on 'palming it'. That's what you call the bit where you hide the coin from your audience without them knowing. They think it's in one hand, but you've already got it in the other. It's the bit that takes the most practice to make it look natural.

'What are you doing?' asked Umer, who was sitting on the bench beside me.

'I can't tell you – it's a secret,' I replied. 'In fact,

it's best you don't even look.'

'Oh,' said Umer, and he turned to stare at his feet. 'So, um . . . how was cricket practice?'

'I don't wanna talk about it,' I muttered.

'Oh . . . right,' replied Umer.

He sat twiddling his thumbs as he searched for something else to talk about.

'Um . . . I had chips for dinner,' he eventually offered.

I looked up at him.

'That's a great story, Umer. You mind if I tell people that story and pretend it's mine?'

'Sure,' he said with a big smile.

Man, I envied Umer sometimes. Not even sarcasm could touch him. I guess my bad mood was mine to keep.

The assembly hall was just starting to sound like a monkey riot, when there came a shout from the stage.

'QUIETEN DOWN!' roared the headmaster.

The effect was impressive. Three hundred kids immediately swallowed their chat, plunging the room into total silence.

'Now,' continued the head, 'as some of you will know already, Mrs Popperkettle, who normally

plays the piano for us during assembly, is off school
with a potentially fatal case of diarrhoea.'

'*YAY!*' came a cheer from the kids.

'QUIET!' roared Mr Offalbox. 'Now, we've
been lucky enough to receive an offer of help from
Mrs Masood, who will be taking Mrs Popperkettle's
place, to lead us in our morning songs.'

The headmaster gestured to one side of the
stage as a colourfully dressed woman stomped
into view carrying an enormous sitar over her
shoulder.

'*Hi-hi-hiii!*' shrieked Mrs Masood as she dumped
the big wooden instrument on the stage beside the
head.

She scanned the crowd for a moment, then called
out, 'Hello, my little poppadom!' to a blushing Year
Three girl in the middle of the room.

The girl gave her an awkward wave in return.

'Ah, yes,' said Mr Offalbox, beaming at her from
the stage. 'Your niece Sumeera is a student here.
Won't it be nice to have your auntie play for us?'

Sumeera nodded and stared at her feet. You got
the impression she'd heard her auntie play before.
I was already dreading it. The sitar Mrs Masood
was carrying looked kind of like a big, bulbous

guitar with a long neck. It had so many strings you couldn't count them. From what I knew, you had to be pretty talented to play one. It didn't take long to confirm that Mrs Masood was not.

The next half hour was genuinely weird. It was like a Spotify playlist that literally no one ever would select: an insane mix of Beatles songs, Christian hymns and Bollywood hits, played by a cheerful fifty-year-old Asian woman on an instrument she had no right owning, let alone performing with. At first, kids tried to sing along with the songs they vaguely recognized. But towards the end everyone just sat in confused silence. Even the headmaster looked like he was trying to remember why he'd accepted the offer.

There was scattered applause when she finished. Mr Offalbox looked relieved as he took his place back at the centre of the stage.

'Right . . .' he began, sounding quieter than normal, 'let's give a big thank-you to Mrs Masood for her . . . um . . . music.'

'*Thaaaankkk yyooouu*,' came the unenthusiastic response from the room.

'Now, before we wrap up,' said Mr Offalbox, 'I want to remind you that there are still places available for the annual school talent show. We really want to get together the best show possible and avoid a repeat of last year's audience walk-outs.'

'What do you think, Humza?' whispered Umer. 'Maybe we could perform the track?'

'At a kids' talent show?' I replied. 'No way! Talent shows are for sell-outs, man! Sure, I could *definitely* win it, but then they'd make me work with Simon Cowell and do a Christmas single. I need my artistic freedom.'

'Oh, right,' replied Umer. 'I hadn't thought of that.'

'Course you hadn't. That's why I'm the brains of this operation and you're the guy who holds my bag while I'm on the toilet.'

'It's nice to be useful,' said Umer with a small smile.

As the day went on, it became clear that it wasn't just Mrs Popperkettle who was missing. Staff were dropping like flies all over the place. Mr Parks, Miss Ofori, dinner ladies Betty and Moira, even Nurse Sue. All of them were off with some illness or accident. We didn't even know what had happened to most of them; though we did hear Mr Parks had been bitten by an escaped bear. That's right, you heard me, a bear! Who gets bitten by a bear in this day and age? The whole thing was just weird. A few teachers not showing up because they're sick or depressed or hung-over, that's to be expected. But this was crazy. I'd never seen so many teachers off at once. And, while that would normally be something to celebrate, there was a disturbing pattern emerging.

Umer was the first to notice it – which was surprising, as normally he's slower than a one-legged tortoise.

'See that woman over there?' he said, pointing to a familiar-looking Asian woman in a bright pink dress.

'Who, that marshmallow-looking one?' I replied.

'Uh-huh. That's Abdullah's Auntie Fatima.'

'Oh yeah. I thought I recognized her. She once made me wash my mouth out with soap after I accidentally swore at their parrot three hundred times.'

'And over there, talking to the headmaster, do you see that woman in the green?'

I looked over to where he was pointing and saw Mr Offalbox talking to another Asian lady in a colourful dress.

'Oh yeah, Mrs Hameed. I've been to their restaurant for Eid.'

'Right, and did you know her nephew Ahmed was in Year Two?' added Umer.

'Course not. I don't talk to Year Twos. What you getting at, man?'

'Well,' Umer continued, 'it's just that all the staff who are off this week seem to have been replaced by local people. And not just normal people . . . local aunties.'

I had a look about. Straight away I spotted one through the window on the second floor, cleaning one of the whiteboards. Then I noticed another in the canteen, sorting cutlery. And coming through the gate, weighed down by bags of groceries, were two more auntie-looking Asian women. All of them were dressed in colourful shalwar kameez dresses. All were round and cuddly. And all of them were related to some kid or other at the school.

'Huh!' I replied. 'There *are* an awful lot of aunties here today. Normally they only gather in these kinds of numbers for a wedding or an open buffet.'

'Yeah,' agreed Umer. 'There's something a bit creepy about it.'

'Well, you know what Asian aunties are like – they love inserting themselves in other people's business. I once had one come to a dentist appointment with me just to watch. Who goes to someone else's dentist appointment? Aunties are weird.'

'Yeah, I guess they're just trying to help out with the staff shortage,' added Umer. 'But it's still strange. I mean . . . they're everywhere you look.'

We sat quietly and took it all in. Pakistani aunties, Indian aunties, Sri Lankan aunties, Bangladeshi aunties, maybe more . . . It was definitely a disturbing number of aunties for a single location. One auntie can be unsettling enough, but a dozen together? That was a herd. A herd of aunties can skeletonize a cow in under a minute. Or maybe that was piranhas . . . Either way, the point still stands. With this many aunties about, you'd better watch your back . . .

After break we had an art lesson with Auntie Uzma. I'm not exaggerating when I say it was the best art lesson ever. I mean, I love art anyway; after music with Mr T, it's probably my favourite lesson of the week. I normally spend all my time drawing secret agents from the PIA shooting each other with laser guns. That's the Pakistani Intelligence Agency, by the way. My dad tried to say that PIA stood for Pakistan International Airlines, but whatever – they probably stole it from me. Anyway, my version's much cooler. They go on missions, save the world, fight bad guys. They're like James Bond but brown.

You can have a look if you like. This one's pretty old, but check it out.

I gotta admit it, that is some strong literature. But today there was no time for PIA comics. Today Auntie Uzma had a special project for us: painting with chocolate.

That's right. Painting. With. Chocolate.

I don't know why I'd even doubted aunties as teachers – this was incredible! No normal teacher would let us do this. Auntie Uzma had brought in this big thing of melted chocolate, and we all got a cup full of it and a fat paintbrush. You could paint whatever you wanted on your paper, but you had to do it quick before the chocolate went hard.

It was pretty difficult with such a big brush and such thick paint, so in the end I just wrote . . .

LITTLE
BADMAN

. . . in delicious chocolate letters, next to a smiley face with my hat on (that's my logo – I was gonna trademark it, but I don't know how).

On his bit of paper, Umer drew a big happy bee. 'That's a nice bee, man,' I told him. 'Is it Mustafa?'

'Yeah, he's happy cos he just stung a teacher on the nose,' replied Umer.

We let our pictures dry in front of the electric fan that Auntie Uzma had brought in specially. Then, once they were hard enough, she showed us how to peel the paper off carefully, so that the chocolate picture came away in one piece.

After that came the best bit. Eating. I tell you, man, art has never tasted so good! All artwork should be made out of chocolate – chocolate statues, chocolate pottery – hell, whole chocolate galleries!

I was gutted when the bell went for lunch. After eating my chocolate masterpiece, I wasn't exactly looking forward to a steaming heap of mystery stew. We trudged into the canteen as usual and took our places in the line.

'I might just have a glass of water,' I said to Umer. 'I don't want to ruin the taste of my artwork.'

'I'm just gonna lick the paper,' he replied, taking out the folded-up sheet he'd used to paint on.

'Is there any chocolate left on it?' I asked.

'No, but you can still smell it a bit,' he said, giving it a sniff.

And that was when it happened. The kid in

front stepped out of the way, revealing before us a sight that would make a hungry dog weep. Food! Mountains of it! And not school food . . . real food! Tasty food. Auntie food!

There was chicken tikka, lamb karahi, pakora, samosas, butter chicken, aloo gobi, prawn curry, laddoo and – yeah, you guessed it – gulab jamun! Behind the stacks of delicious dinners and desserts stood three brightly dressed aunties, working like machines to serve every kid who stepped up to the counter; heaping on extra-tall helpings, so heavy you needed both hands to lift them.

'Umer . . .' I said, my mouth hanging open like an idiot goldfish, '. . . it's beautiful.'

'I'm getting seconds!' he gasped. 'No, thirds!'

I'm not ashamed to say we got well and truly stuck in. Umer and I can hold our own in an eating contest, but, I tell you, we outdid ourselves that day. Maybe it was all the months of mystery stew, haddock surprise, or that nut roast made out of tree bark, but we ate like it was our last meal. Whoever had the idea of swapping dinner ladies with aunties was a genius.

'*Umbah,*' I said to Umer with a full mouth, '*dis ib amabing!*'

'*UH-HUNH!*' he agreed with a full mouth of his own.

It was a good day. Maybe the best day. Nothing – and I mean *nothing* – could wipe the smile off my face. Not the cricket team, not my dad, not even Mr Gibbs, the deputy headmaster, being escorted off the premises by the police (apparently, he'd been stealing garden gnomes all over town and would need to be replaced by a suitably qualified auntie). As I wandered back to class in a daze, my stomach was too full for me to worry about any of it.

I had definitely got these aunties all wrong. Yeah, it was weird but weird ain't always bad. They were just stepping up, helping out, looking after *us*, the next generation. And they were doing it in classic auntie style: food, food and more food. Between this and the work we were doing on my music track, truth was, school had never been better.

Yeah, cricket practice still sucked worse than a vacuum cleaner full of leeches but, with a bit of luck, the team would mutiny before long and kick Dad out. Then I'd be free to quit.

I was heading back inside when I ran into Mr Turnbull pinning a photocopied sheet to the student notice board.

'Hey, Mr T,' I said, slapping him on the back. 'If you ain't had your lunch yet, do yourself a favour and get down to the canteen. I must have had six helpings. Even my shadow's put on a stone.'

'Sounds good,' said Mr Turnbull. 'But my wife's got me on a health kick.'

'You've got a wife? Weird. I figured you just had cats or a big DVD collection or something.'

'Nope,' he said with a smile, and he pointed to a ring on his left hand. 'Found someone who'd have me.'

'Well, they do say there's someone for everyone. Even bald guys in sandals. She must be a real special lady.'

'Uh-huh, I'm very lucky,' he replied, laughing. 'So what do you think — are you going to enter the talent show?'

Mr Turnbull nodded towards the poster he'd just put up. It had a cartoon of a kid on it, standing on stage singing. Below that, there was a box for you to sign your name in if you wanted to take part.

'Ah, man,' I replied, shaking my head. 'Are you pushing that too? I already told Umer, I ain't gonna sell out with some talent show.'

'Why on earth would it be selling out?'

'You know, getting up in front of the judges with some sob story — "Hi, my name's Humza and I started rapping when my cat died of feline diabetes." I ain't into all that. I'm all about the music, son.'

'I know you're serious about your music, Humza, but this could be a good opportunity to practise performing to a crowd. It's harder than it looks. And don't call me "son".'

'Sorry, sir. It's just not my thing, you know? Thanks for the heads-up though.'

'No problem. Are you looking forward to doing some more work on your track tomorrow?'

'Ah, yeah! I can't wait. Maybe you can send the rest of the class out to count clouds or something, so we can get some proper work done.'

'We'll see,' he said with a smile, before turning and heading back to his room.

If I'd known then what I know now, I'd have followed him. I wouldn't have let him out of my sight. Maybe I could have stopped it? Maybe I could have helped? But how was I to know that the same thing that was happening to all the other teachers at my school was about to happen to Mr Turnbull . . . ?

CHAPTER SIX
THE GRANDPA SITUATION

It was about twenty past three when I let myself in at Grandpa's house. Mum had given me the key so she wouldn't have to bother coming round again. Pretty lazy if you ask me. But I suppose she does do all my cooking and cleaning and laundry – so I'll give her a pass this time.

As usual, Grandpa was nowhere to be seen.

'Yo, Grandpa! David Chesterton! Where you at?' I called.

There was no answer. I dumped my school bag in the hall and walked into the living room. I figured they'd be curled up together in their usual spot. But when I got there all I found was a grandpa-shaped dent in the sofa.

'Hello?' I said more quietly.

Still no answer. I checked the kitchen, the dining

room – no sign of them. It looked like Auntie Uzma had been busy though. There were pots and pans everywhere. And food. So much food. Cakes, pastries, pies. She was in cooking overdrive. I guess she needed to unwind after a hard day's teaching or something, but this seemed a bit mental. I mean, she could have catered for a wedding with the amount of food she had in that kitchen.

And if you've ever been to an Asian wedding you'll know what I'm talking about. They have so many guests even the bride and groom don't know half of 'em. Second cousins, third cousins, fourth cousins, former neighbours, ex-doctors, childhood postmen – everyone your family ever met, lived near or shared a lift with is there. And they all want feeding. Hell, half the time they're only there for the food.

And Auntie Uzma could have done it with this lot. It was like she was getting ready for the apocalypse. Making sure she and Grandpa would have enough food to last them to the year 3000. It goes without saying that I helped myself to a gulab jamun or two. It's what Auntie would have wanted. And it's not like anyone would have missed them – there were, like, seven hundred of the things just sitting there on the counter.

I munched one down as I walked upstairs.

'Gwampar?' I called out with a full mouth. 'Dabid Chestertom?'

Still no answer. I checked the bedrooms, the bathroom, the airing cupboard. No sign of Grandpa or David Chesterton anywhere. Then I had an idea.

I fetched a chair from the bedroom and, climbing on to it, hooked a finger into the loop hanging down from the loft hatch. As it creaked open, two faces appeared in the darkness above. One belonged to a fluffy, overfed cat, and the other to the oldest uncle in the universe.

'All right, Grandpa,' I said, smiling up at him. 'What you doing in the loft?'

'What do you think, David Chesterton?' asked Grandpa. 'Can we trust him?'

David Chesterton stared at me long and hard.

'*Purr-rrp*,' he replied, then turned away, walking back into the attic.

Grandpa smiled.

'Hello, boy,' he said, and lowered the ladder.

Up in the loft, I took a seat beside Grandpa on the floor. I figured he might explain what he was doing up there, but, instead, he just sat staring at me.

'So, uh . . .' I began, 'why you in the loft, Uncle? You been practising magic tricks?'

He didn't smile, just leaned in close, with this intense look.

'Hiding,' he whispered.

'Hiding? What you hiding from?'

'That creature,' he replied.

'Creature? There's a creature in the house? Damn, man, why'd no one tell me? I could have been eaten!'

'It's gone out,' he replied matter-of-factly.

'Gone out? Then let's go lock the door!'

'It has a key,' said Grandpa, as though this was obvious.

'A creature with a key? Does Auntie Uzma know?'

He gave me a weird look, like I was the confused one.

'Auntie Uzma *is* the creature,' he whispered.

'Huh? What you talking about, Grandpa?'

'Auntie Uzma is not Auntie Uzma,' he said, leaning in. 'It is an imposter.'

'An imposter?' I replied, raising my eyebrows and looking over at David Chesterton, to see if he also thought Grandpa might be losing it. 'I see . . .'

'I am not mad!' snapped Grandpa.

'Hey, no one said you were mad,' I replied in my best calming voice. 'It just all sounds a bit . . . you know . . . mad.'

'That *thing*, cooking, cooking, cooking all the time! That is not my wife!' barked Grandpa.

'Right, well if it ain't Auntie Uzma, then you must have got an upgrade, cos that thing sure can cook. I've never seen so much tasty food! Maybe we can swap my mum out for one of them too?'

'This is not funny,' said Grandpa, and I could see he meant it.

'Grandpa, man. It *is* your wife. It *is* Auntie Uzma. I spent the whole day with her at school. She's just the same as always.'

'I knew you would not believe me,' he said, shaking his head. 'Only David Chesterton sees it.'

David Chesterton gave me a pretty severe look for a cat. I didn't know what to say. I mean, this was properly crazy. Grandpa had always seemed pretty together mentally. I know old people sometimes get confused, but Grandpa wasn't that kind of old person. He was the other kind that can't open jars.

We sat in silence for a while after that. I wasn't really sure how to respond to the whole 'imposter auntie' bit. I mean, what do you say to something like that? As a kid, it was a bit above my level of expertise.

'I've been practising,' I said, slipping the old coin from my pocket. I showed him my best attempt at the disappearing coin trick. It wasn't perfect yet, but it wasn't bad either. Grandpa smiled a small smile as he watched me.

'Good,' he said after a time. 'Good.'

It was all he said.

We didn't learn any more tricks that day. I sat and practised the coin trick in silence until Auntie Uzma came home. I thought about telling her what Grandpa had told me, but decided against it. Better just to leave them to sort it out themselves.

I felt a bit sad walking home that afternoon. I realized I'd actually kinda been looking forward to hanging out with Grandpa. This just wasn't the same. Damn.

Back at school the next day, Auntie Uzma was upping her game yet again. She'd come up with a brand-new lesson idea: cake review! I'm not too proud of myself when I say that I totally forgot about the whole Grandpa situation the moment Auntie Uzma dropped that fat slice of cake on my desk.

'Pinch me, Umer,' I murmured. 'I don't think I've woken up yet.'

'Can't . . .' he replied. 'I'm dreaming too. Chocolate double fudge . . .' he moaned. He was actually drooling.

When she'd finished giving everyone a slice, Auntie Uzma turned and faced the class.

'OK, my beautiful, cuddly kiddiewinks!' she said with a giggle. 'Today we will be reviewing Auntie Uzma's chocolate double-fudge gâteau.'

The class cheered. Only Wendy Wang looked puzzled. She raised her hand and waited to be called on.

'Yes, Wendy?' said Auntie Uzma.

'I was just wondering,' she said, lowering her hand. 'What's the academic merit of this lesson?'

'Cake,' replied Auntie Uzma with a big grin.

Again the class cheered.

'Sure,' said Wendy, forcing an awkward smile. 'I enjoy cake as much as the next student, but I don't understand how we're learning anything from eating it.'

'Quiet, Wendy!' I shouted across the room. 'Why

would you argue with cake?'

'Educational value aside,' continued Wendy, 'I'm just not sure it's all that healthy.'

'Right!' snapped Auntie Uzma, the smile vanishing from her face. 'That's enough of that kind of talk. Go to the headmaster this instant!'

The class gasped. Wendy Wang was getting sent to the headmaster? I'd known Wendy for as long as I could remember, and that had never, never ever, ever happened before. Ever!

'Excuse me?' said Wendy, like her brain genuinely couldn't compute what she'd just heard.

'I will not put up with this kind of disruptive behaviour,' continued Auntie Uzma. 'You will spend the lesson with the headmaster and stay behind after school. For double cake review!'

I'd never seen Auntie Uzma look so strict. She was actually a bit scary. Wendy had gone as white as a sheet. Everyone sat quietly as Wendy pushed her chair out with a noisy squeak and made her way to the door.

'I was just . . .' she began.

'Go!' shouted Auntie Uzma.

Wendy pulled the door closed behind her without another word. A moment passed in total, stunned silence. Then Auntie Uzma turned back to face us with an enormous, happy grin.

'OK then, my chubby little beauties!' she said. 'Dig in!'

Slowly, one by one, the class began to eat their slices of cake. Little whispered conversations began to spring up around the class and, though I couldn't hear them all, I knew they were about Wendy.

'What was that about?' whispered Umer, as he plucked off a hunk of cake between his finger and thumb.

'I don't know, man,' I replied. 'I've never seen her snap like that before. I mean, she can be grumpy, but that was pretty severe. I don't think Wendy's ever been sent to the headmaster.'

It was weird, but I found myself feeling a bit sorry for her. Normally Wendy's just there to grass on me or make me look stupid in tests. Usually I'd be all on board with her getting in trouble. But now that it had happened, it just felt a bit . . . unfair.

Oh well, it was still pretty good cake. I was confident that I wouldn't worry about it for long. And I didn't.

★

Two hours later Umer and I were running down the hall as fast as we could go. We weren't after a good place in the lunch queue this time – we were heading to our music lesson!

Today was the big day. The day I was gonna lay down my new vocals. I'd been working on them whenever I got a chance – though that seemed less and less of the time, what with Grandpa and cricket and all the eating I'd been doing. But it didn't matter: my lyrics were perfect now. They were ready to go.

'I've got a good feeling about today,' I said to Umer as we tore up the stairs towards Mr Turnbull's room. 'I think we might finally get this track locked down.' I was pretty sure Mr T would be as excited as we were.

We skidded to a stop outside his room, out of breath and grinning like idiots. We had arrived well ahead of the rest of the class, which meant we could set up in peace. The door was closed, which I knew meant Mr Turnbull was taking today seriously as well. He was probably already in there setting up microphones and doing sound checks.

I turned the door handle and walked in.

'Yo, yo, yo! Little Badman in the house!' I said,

stepping through the door, eyes closed, head back and hands in the air, like I was walking on stage to the cries of a thousand star-struck fans.

But when I opened my eyes there was no Mr Turnbull. No recording equipment. Nothing but a sizeable Pakistani lady in a fluorescent green shalwar kameez. She was sitting on a child-sized stool in the centre of the room, smiling.

'Jelly Baby?' she said, holding out a little white paper bag full of sweets.

'Uh . . . where's Mr Turnbull?' I asked.

'Oh, poor man,' said the woman. 'He has gone loopy-loopy-mad and lost his job.'

'*Loopy-loopy-mad?* What you talking about? Mr Turnbull ain't mad,' I told her.

'Oh, I'm afraid he is. Yes, yes, he is,' she replied with that same weird smile. 'That poor man is wearing shoes on his hands and gloves on his feet, and a hat glued to his *bottom*, of all places.'

'What?' I cried. 'He ain't done that! You're making it up!'

'Why would I make it up? I am just here to help,' she said, still smiling, still holding out the bag of Jelly Babies. 'So many ill teachers right now, so much misfortune in one school. Thank goodness for all the local aunties, offering to help.'

'But what about my track? We're meant to record it today!'

'Oh no, no,' she replied. 'Today we are singing songs about delicious food, and then we are trying those foods, and then we are singing more songs and eating more foods! Won't it be wonderful?'

'What is it with you and food?' I yelled. 'I get it: aunties like feeding people, but this is getting ridiculous!'

'Hey!' she suddenly snapped. 'We will have none of that kind of talk! We aunties are here out of the kindness of our hearts. But if you continue with that I will send you straight to the headmaster.'

'Don't even worry about it,' I said. 'I'm going there anyway! Come on, Umer.'

'Can I have a Jelly Baby?' asked Umer.

'No!' I snapped, grabbing him by the arm and dragging him off in the direction of the headmaster's room.

Mr Offalbox was sitting behind his desk when we ran in. Actually, he was sort of sitting all around it. He was so big for the room he had to lean forward a little so he didn't bang his head on the bookshelves behind him.

His great big gorilla arms covered most of the surface area of the desk, making his laptop look like a birthday card. He hunched over the tiny machine like he was guarding it from being stolen by other, smaller apes.

'In trouble again, are you?' he said before I could speak.

'No!' I replied, offended. 'I mean, yeah, I suppose, but I'd have come here anyway.'

'What's all this about, boys? I've already had Wendy Wang writing lines in the corner all morning. That was unsettling enough for one day.'

'Where's Mr Turnbull?' I demanded. 'There's some weird old auntie in his room.'

'Ah, yes. You're quite fond of Mr Turnbull, aren't you, Humza?' he said, nodding his head. 'Well, your concern is appreciated. I had a call from his doctor this morning. She explained that he's not been doing too well. He's been suffering from nervous exhaustion and will be requiring some time away from work.'

'Nervous exhaustion?' I replied. 'Have you met him? Nothing fazes that man. I've seen sloths more uptight.'

'Nonetheless, he's been under rather a lot of pressure apparently and will need to recuperate at home for a time. Thankfully, though, Mrs Jahib has been kind enough to step in and fill his position for the time being. She has some truly original ideas about combining music with food. So hurry back to class or you'll miss out.'

'But . . .' I protested.

'No, Humza – now!' snapped Mr Offalbox.

It was useless. He wasn't listening. Umer and I

trudged back to class in stunned silence.

It was the worst music lesson ever. Worse than that. Worse than detention, mystery stew and not having a proper phone combined. The other kids seemed to enjoy it somehow. They were playing stupid songs about food on their recorders and tambourines, then eating whatever they'd sung about.

Mrs Jahib had brought in a whole suitcase of diffcrent treats. But I wasn't hungry. I just sat at the back and shook my head. Why did no one care about Mr Turnbull?

'This is terrible,' I said to Umer.

'Uh-huh,' he agreed, then continued work on his song about doughnuts.

'What are you doing, man?' I snapped at him. 'Stop supporting this! You're betraying Mr T!'

'I'm just doing what the teacher asked,' said Umer, looking a bit hurt by my accusation.

'She ain't a teacher. She's some kid's auntie. She's only qualified to cook daal, pinch cheeks and make older cousins feel bad they ain't married yet. She definitely ain't no Mr Turnbull.'

'I'm not saying she is, but what can we do?' asked Umer.

'I don't know yet,' I replied, staring hard at Mrs Jahib. 'But I'm gonna figure it out.'

As I walked out the school gates that afternoon, with my head down, I reminded myself that the only good thing about such a terrible day was that it definitely, absolutely, without doubt couldn't get any worse . . . And then Dad grabbed me by the collar and yanked me into a minivan.

I thought I was being kidnapped for a second, until I saw the rest of the cricket team in the back. My dad might try to kidnap one or two kids at once, but not twelve. There must be something else going on.

'What the hell, man?' I yelled. 'What are you doing?'

'Cricket match!' said my dad with a grin. 'We are late!'

He slammed his foot down on the accelerator and we took off like a rocket. I barely managed to get my seat belt on as we tore out of the school lane and into the high street, narrowly missing an old lady and her terrified dog. I was pretty used to my dad's terrible driving, but the rest of the team had no idea what was going on. They were doing their best just to stay inside the vehicle. Cricket equipment and school bags were flying about all over the place as the van bounced round corners and over hills. Kids screamed and turned green as we raced through the streets at breakneck speed.

'Slow down, Dad!' I shouted. 'You're gonna get us all killed!'

'I *will* slow down,' he shouted back, 'after we get there!'

I was pretty sure he was enjoying this. I mean, why wouldn't he be? He was combining his three favourite things: driving badly, cricket and ruining my life.

'Humza!' shouted Jamal Jones from the back. 'Tell your dad we're sorry. Tell him we'll behave and do whatever he tells us if he just stops the van.'

'Sorry, Jamal,' I shouted back at him. 'He won't listen to me. All we can do is pray for a quick death.'

But a quick death didn't come. Somehow we managed to get there in one piece with only Imran Yusuf losing his lunch. Unfortunately, he'd had second helpings of kheer for dessert, so it wasn't a pretty sight. (Picture a kind of rice pudding that already looked like sick before you ate it. Now picture it all over a minivan and you get the idea.)

We staggered out of the van like a dozen four-foot zombies and collapsed on the grass. You had to give it to my dad: having learned to drive on the streets of Karachi, he could handle himself behind the wheel. Don't get me wrong, it was a horrible experience – I'd rather eat a book than go on a driving holiday with him – *but*, if you've got to do some dangerous driving, he's your man.

By the time Imran had finished throwing up, Dad had found where we were meant to be playing and began shepherding the team towards the cricket field. I say 'cricket field'; it was more like an area of dirt where slightly less of the grass was dead. Like a filthy little oasis, in a *really* filthy desert.

'What is this place?' I asked my dad.

'This is the other school's playing field,' he said, sounding excited.

'What school?' I asked, starting to feel nervous.

'Grungle's Academy,' he replied.

'You what?' I cried. 'Lester Grungle's Academy for Aggressive Boys? Are you insane?'

'Do not be such an elderly woman,' replied Dad, shaking his head.

'Have you even heard of this place?' I said, desperate to talk some sense into him. 'Rumour is they ate one of their dinner ladies! The school motto is "A punch in the face". Even the teachers are on day release from prison. We can't play them! We shouldn't even be here!'

'Sounds like someone has pre-game nerves to me,' chuckled Dad.

'I've got pre-getting-murdered nerves!' I yelled, but he wasn't listening.

'Ah, here they come now,' he said with a broad smile.

The rest of our team had fallen silent. I turned to see what everyone was staring at. The other school were making their way across the wasteland towards us. Damn . . . I've never seen an under-twelve with a beard, but somehow they'd found one. They had one kid who was over six feet, another kid who was built like a fridge, one with facial tattoos and another half dozen or so who could have been extras in *Mad Max*.

'OK,' said Dad cheerfully. 'Time to get changed.'

'What?' I cried. 'Where?'

'Right here.'

'Here? There ain't no changing rooms here!'

'You don't need changing room,' he said, shaking his head. 'No one is watching. No one cares.'

'What? What about the psychos on the other team? They're watching!'

'Don't be so stupid, boy!' said my dad. 'They are professional young men. They will not laugh. Now strip to your knickers!'

This sucked so, so, so, so, so, so, so bad. I can't tell you how bad this sucked. The other team began to crack up almost immediately as we started getting into our cricket gear. They were pointing at us and making comments.

I felt like an idiot. My dad didn't seem to notice. He was just talking to their teacher. I say 'teacher' – he looked like a gang leader. He had an eyepatch, a ton of piercings and chunks shaved out of his hair, seemingly at random.

When we were changed, a few members of the other team walked over to us.

'Uh . . . all right?' I said to the bearded guy.

He stared at me like I was roadkill.

'We hate cricket,' he said in a voice much too deep for any twelve-year-old. 'We hate cricket so much.'

'Ah, man! Me too!' I replied, relieved that we had something in common.

'They make us play it for discipline,' said the guy who looked like a fridge.

'They make *me* play it for discipline too!' I told him, excited by the thought that we might get along after all.

'It fills us with anger,' added the facial tattoo guy. 'We're going to take that anger out on you.'

'Oh . . . ' I replied, the excitement fading from my voice.

'Come on, son,' called my dad from over by the stumps. 'Stop making boyfriends. Time for cricket!'

'Ah, man,' I groaned. 'Please don't listen to anything that guy says. He ain't stable.'

'Is that your dad?' asked bearded guy.

'Uh . . . yeah, but only biologically.'

'Then this is on you,' he said, giving me a long, hard, bearded stare, before walking away with the rest of the team.

'Why does everyone keep saying that?' I cried.

'I think you just made another enemy,' said Jamal Jones, bumping my shoulder as he walked past me and on to the field.

For the first time since this had all begun, I was grateful we were playing cricket. Don't get me wrong, I still hated cricket, but at least it wasn't football or rugby. Imagine if we were up against these guys in a rugby match. I'd spend the next year in hospital if I was lucky. But, with cricket, at least you barely get anywhere near each other. How much damage could they really do to me? It would probably all just be insults and intimidation.

And then they bowled the first ball. I say 'bowled', but this wasn't any type of bowling that's ever been seen in cricket before. It was more like they loaded a cannon and fired it into my face. I was up to bat first, and their bowler was the guy who looked like a fridge. I've never seen such muscles on a kid. His bicep was as big as my chest. When he threw that ball – overarm and with all his force – I didn't even see it fly. One second it was in his hand, the next second the whole world turned black . . .

★

When I came to, the first thing I was aware of was terrible music. Real wedding party stuff. Had I fallen asleep at a wedding? I couldn't remember. If it *was* a wedding, they had an awful singer.

I opened my eyes to see Dad on the seat next to me in the van, singing at the top of his lungs. He looked happy. More than happy . . . *excited*. Then it all began to come back to me. The cricket match, the other school, the opening bowl . . .

'What happened?' I murmured.

'Oh, he is awake!' shouted my dad over the music.

'What's going on? Why are you happy?' I asked.

'We won!' he replied. 'We beat the other team!'

That didn't make any sense at all. What had I missed? I looked back and saw the rest of our team in the van behind me. They weren't celebrating like my dad was. They looked pretty miserable. And they all had big round bruises on their foreheads. I touched my head lightly.

'Ow!' I cried.

Looking in the wing mirror, I saw that I had a big red welt of my own right there in the centre of my forehead.

'The other team were disqualified for disorderly

conduct,' said my dad with a big smile. 'We won by default!'

'Default?' I said, still feeling confused.

'But it is *still* a win!' snapped my dad. 'I told you I would coach you to victory!'

So this was what winning felt like. Hmm . . . I wasn't sure I liked it after all. My head hurt, my teammates hated me and my dad had stolen all the glory for himself. All in all, this had been a pretty terrible day.

'Who wants to go for UFC? My treat!' shouted Dad over his shoulder to the rest of the team.

'Ultimate Fighting Championships?' asked Jamal, sounding surprised.

'What? No!' replied Dad. 'Uzbek Fried Chicken! Half the price of upmarket brand.'

There were some uncertain murmurs from the back seats, which my dad took as a yes.

We sat in silence at the Uzbek Fried Chicken restaurant, eating the greasy meals that we'd had to pay for ourselves, cos one of the kids from the academy had stolen my dad's wallet. I found myself wondering if this was what rock bottom felt like.

Turned out it wasn't even close.

CHAPTER SEVEN
AUNTIES, AUNTIES EVERYWHERE

My forehead was still throbbing the next day as I sat in the canteen, finishing a third helping of biryani.

'I just have to keep reminding myself,' I told Umer, 'it's all worth it for that camera. What's a small concussion in the grand scale of things?'

'Exactly,' he replied with a warm smile. 'And that bruise will only look stupid for, like, a week or something.'

I could tell he was genuinely trying to be supportive, so I didn't flick food at him, but it took a lot of self-control.

'The only thing is though,' he continued, 'even if we *do* get the camera now, we haven't got any music. And without Mr Turnbull's help we're not going to get any anytime soon.'

He was right. Without Mr T we were stuck . . . And then something struck me. Not about the track. I mean it literally hit me in the back of the head.

'Ow!' I yelled, as whatever it was pinged off my ear and landed in my food.

I turned round to see who'd done it, but there was no one there.

'What the . . .' I muttered.

I looked back down at the table and saw a button lying in my biryani.

'Where'd that come from?' I asked, just as another one whizzed past my nose and straight into Roberta Glott's chocolate milkshake.

I looked over to see a group of kids laughing their heads off. Sitting in the middle of them was Bilal Bashir. He was sucking in his tummy as far as he could, then letting it go all at once. His belly bounced forward with such force it stretched the front of his shirt to bursting point.

PING! Another button tore from his top and fired across the room. The group surrounding him all screamed with laughter again. He'd lost so many buttons now that you could see his belly button staring out through the little gap in his shirt. He really could do with a larger size.

And that was when I noticed it. Looking around the room, I realized that all the school uniforms seemed a bit on the small side – a little tighter than they used to.

'Huh,' I said to Umer. 'You know what . . . I think everyone's clothes have shrunk.'

He looked up from his spoonful of sticky toffee pudding and nodded. 'I see what you mean,' he said. 'Mine have been feeling a bit tight lately too.'

And it wasn't just the other kids. Now that I thought about it, I hadn't had to wear a belt for a few days either. What a weird coincidence. Everybody's clothes shrinking at the same time. It could mean only one thing. Careless laundry! I would definitely have to have a word with Mum when I got home. How hard can it be to wash some clothes? I'd do it myself if it wasn't so boring.

As we walked back to class, we passed Mr Turnbull's room. The door was open and inside we could see Mrs Jahib handing out a toffee apple and a kazoo to each of the nursery kids.

'Man,' I said to Umer, 'I wish I knew where

Mr T lived so we could go round and see what's happened to him.'

'Yeah,' agreed Umer. 'It does seem a bit out of character for him to suddenly go crazy.'

'And, even if he is off his rocker, maybe his wife would still let us use his laptop for a bit? Just to get a copy of the track.'

'I doubt it,' said Umer.

'Yeah, she'd probably just think we wanted to nick it.'

'No, I mean she doesn't have it. See?' said Umer, pointing into the classroom.

And there it was. High up on the shelf, where Mr Turnbull always stored it for safekeeping, was his laptop. No one had touched it. Little round Mrs Jahib probably couldn't even see it from her perspective.

'Umer! You're a genius!' I cried.

'Thanks,' said Umer, beaming at the compliment.

'We've got to get hold of it!'

'Are you sure we're allowed? I mean, it *is* still staff property,' said Umer, sounding nervous.

'Of course I'm sure! It's what Mr Turnbull would want. He knows we were on the brink of stardom. Do you think he'd want us to lose everything just cos he lost his marbles?'

'I guess not,' agreed Umer.

'Exactly. Which is why we need to steal it. And *that's* gonna call for a diversion.'

Thankfully, I had just the thing . . .

Half an hour later the nursery music lesson was in full swing. The kids were making a horrible din with their kazoos. It sounded like a rave in a beehive. I flung open the door with as much drama as possible and leapt into the classroom. The horrible noise came to a sudden stop, as every kid in the room turned to face me.

'Miss!' I shouted. 'We need to evacuate the school! There's a . . . g-g-ghost!'

I've got to admit, it was a pretty good performance. I'm kind of a natural, actually. After I've won all the music awards going, I must remember to make time to pick up an Oscar.

Anyway, nobody moved an inch, though a few of the youngest kids began to look a bit nervous.

'What is this about?' demanded Mrs Jahib. 'Get out of this classroom and stop wasting our time!'

I knew there might be resistance at first; I'd planned for it. That's when phase two of the plan kicked in. It started as a terrifying howl . . .

'*Ooo-oohhhhhhhh . . .*' came a voice from beyond the door.

Everybody turned to look. I took a step into the room . . . a step closer to the laptop.

'*Woo-ooohhhhh . . . Waa-aaahhhh!*' moaned the voice, louder and closer with every moment.

'Is it a ghost?' asked a little girl with blonde pigtails, tears beginning to well up in her eyes.

'Uh . . . yeah,' I replied, feeling just a tiny bit bad for the first time.

Maybe this wasn't the ideal plan after all. I didn't want to give a bunch of five-year-olds nightmares. Oh well, it was too late for that now. And that's when it appeared!

'*Woo-ooooo!*' cried Umer, stepping into the room. He had a sheet hanging over him, which we'd nicked from Nurse Sue's room, and he was holding his hands out wide, classic ghost style. I knew that when the screaming started I'd have my chance to grab the laptop.

But the screaming never came. Instead, the little girl with the watery eyes began to giggle. And then she started to laugh. Then they all started to laugh. Thirty little five-year-olds began to crack up at the terrifying spectacle of Umer with a sheet on his head.

'*Woo?*' said Umer, starting to sound a bit less sure of himself. The kids began to jump up from their seats and run over to him, tugging on his sheet, laughing and shouting.

'Aargh! Get off!' shouted Umer, but they wouldn't let go.

'What are you doing?' cried Mrs Jahib. 'Get out of my classroom, this instant!'

But no one was listening. They were all tugging at Umer, pulling him this way and that. One little boy was trying to climb on him; another was kicking him in the shin. Poor Umer was screaming now. He couldn't see a thing.

'Get off me!' he shouted. 'I've made a mistake! I'm not a ghost! Aargh!'

But the kids didn't care. They were loving it. Nursery school kids are basically no different from maximum security prisoners. All it takes is one little spark and you've got a riot on your hands.

For just a moment Umer managed to pull free from most of the group. Still blinded by the sheet, he dived for the door, missed it and crashed into a wall. The shelving above him collapsed. Books and musical instruments rained down on him, hitting him over the head and knocking him off balance.

And that's when the top shelf came loose, spilling its contents everywhere. Mr Turnbull's laptop was sent flying into the air. Everything went into slow motion. If I didn't reach it in the next second, that computer was gonna be scrap metal.

I dived, leaping over the heads of a dozen screaming five-year-olds, bouncing off a tiny chair and throwing myself in the direction of the delicate little machine that held the key to my whole future . . .

An inch from the floor, my fingers wrapped around it, tugging it away from impact. I pulled it to my chest, turned my body so that my shoulder slammed into the ground, and tumbled out the door and into the corridor. When I stood up, I couldn't believe that the laptop and I were both in one piece. Sadly, the same couldn't be said of Umer. He was lying in a heap on the floor, covered in books, recorders and ukuleles, with two dozen kids jumping on him and pulling his hair.

'Oh, hi, Mr Offalbox!' I yelled, looking down the corridor.

All the little rioters froze like statues and looked up at me. Even at that age, they knew that Mr Offalbox was an ogre you didn't mess with.

'Run!' I shouted at Umer.

It took Umer a second to realize that there was no Mr Offalbox and that this was just a diversion. But when he did twig he jumped to his feet and tore out of the door with me. We could hear Mrs Jahib shouting after us as we disappeared round the corner, in search of a quiet place to examine our prize.

★

We were both out of breath when we sat down in the library and opened up the laptop. The screen pinged to life. A little white box appeared, above which was written the word PASSWORD.

'OK, Umer, what's his password?' I asked.

'What?' replied Umer. 'How should I know?'

'Ah, man!' I yelled, probably a bit louder than I should have.

'*SHH!*' came an irritable voice from somewhere in the library.

'I can't believe we've got this far and we don't have the password!' I whispered.

'Maybe we could guess it?' said Umer.

'Good idea! OK, what stuff does Mr T like?' I said.

We stared at each other silently for a moment, thinking it through.

'Socks and sandals!' we both shouted at once.

'*SHHHH!*' came that voice again.

We just ignored it and began typing. I finished entering 'socks and sandals' into the password box and hit GO.

'Incorrect password,' came the response on the screen. 'Two more attempts.'

'"Two more attempts"!' I cried. 'How we gonna

guess it in two more attempts?'

'*SHUUUSSSSSSHHHHHHH!*' came the voice for a third time.

'You shush!' I shouted back, then turned to Umer. 'We'll never guess it in only two goes!'

'What happens if we get it wrong?' asked Umer.

'You get locked out,' replied Wendy Wang, who'd appeared behind us from out of nowhere.

'Wendy Wang!' I said. 'Are you the one that's been shushing us?'

'Well, you are in a library,' answered Wendy, shaking her head. 'Some of us are trying to study. It's not like I can do it in class any more. All we do is eat.'

'It's true,' I replied. 'Those aunties are obsessed.'

'Whose laptop is this?' asked Wendy, looking suspicious.

'Mr Turnbull's,' replied Umer.

'Shut up, Umer!' I snapped. 'Don't tell Wendy Wang. She'll get us in trouble.'

'I don't just tell on everyone, you know!' said Wendy, looking offended.

'You kind of do,' I replied.

'Only when they're breaking the rules,' she said.

'Sometimes you gotta break the rules, Wendy.

It's part of being a kid.'

'And doing the right thing is part of being a grown-up,' replied Wendy, holding her ground. 'When are *you* gonna grow up, Humza?'

'Ha! Have you ever even *met* a grown-up?' I said, laughing. 'They're worse than we are! Take these aunties. They act all sweet, bring us nice food, say that they're helping out with the staff shortage, but there's something weird going on. I can't work out what yet, but something ain't right.'

'Mmm,' replied Wendy, sounding like she might have had the same thought. 'Why have you got Mr Turnbull's laptop then?' she asked.

'Cos he's gone missing and we need a file off it,' I replied.

It was too late to lie to Wendy; might as well come clean.

'Right – well, guessing his password will be next to impossible,' said Wendy, leaning in to examine the laptop. 'You'll need to find a back door into the system. Let me have a look.'

'What, you mean you actually want to help us?' I asked, surprised by her sudden turnaround.

'Not even slightly,' replied Wendy. 'I need to check it out for myself. If it ends up helping you, that's purely a coincidence.'

'But why do you want to see what's on Mr Turnbull's laptop?' asked Umer.

'Because he's one of the ones who've gone missing,' replied Wendy. 'There's something very strange going on in this school and I'm going to get to the bottom of it. A staff laptop might provide just the clue.'

'Whoa! Check you out, Miss Rule Breaker,' I said, patting her on the back.

'I'm not a rule breaker,' snapped Wendy. 'I'm a concerned citizen. When all this is resolved, I shall be informing the headmaster of my actions and will accept any punishment he deems suitable.'

'Yeah, OK, but maybe don't mention us. Me and Umer are on pretty thin ice with Offalbox as it is.'

'Not my concern,' replied Wendy.

'Right. Course not. What was I thinking?' I said, shaking my head.

Wendy snapped shut the laptop and slid it into her bag.

'I'll need to take this home with me,' she said.

'Handling stolen goods, Wendy? That's a felony, you know?' I said, grinning at her.

'We don't have felonies in this country,' replied

Wendy, walking away. 'You watch too much television.'

And then she was gone.

'Do you think we can trust her?' I asked Umer as we made our way out of school that afternoon.

'Who, Wendy?' he replied. 'Yeah, I reckon. I mean, if she was going to stitch us up, wouldn't she have done it already?'

'I guess. She definitely ain't a fan of these aunties.'

'Hi, Auntie,' said Umer, out of nowhere.

'Eh?' I replied, before I realized he wasn't talking to me.

'Ooooooh! My little Umer-bear!' said a great big lady in a turquoise shalwar kameez, as she bent down and gave Umer an enormous cuddle.

'Hey, I know you,' I said to her. 'You're always at Umer's birthdays.'

'This is my Auntie Parveen,' said Umer, wriggling his way out of the powerful bear hug.

'Uh-uh-uh!' she said with a big grin. 'Not *just* Auntie Parveen. Now school nurse Parveen also!'

'What, you work here too?' I said. 'Damn, man. Soon there ain't gonna be no real staff left.'

'Ah, you must be Humza?' said the auntie

nurse. 'I know your mother.'

'Yeah, you aunties all seem to know each other. It's kinda creepy.'

'I will call round and see her later. Bring her some delicious nihari. That poor woman is so thin.'

'Yeah, great, you do that,' I told her, keen to get away.

'See you soon, Auntie,' said Umer, as I dragged him down the hall. 'Thanks again for the bee.'

'Huh?' I said as we rounded the corner. 'What do you mean, thanks for the bee?'

'Mustafa,' replied Umer, like it was obvious.

'Mustafa?'

'Yeah, Auntie Parveen gave him to me as a present. Said I should take him in for show and tell.'

'Wait, so you didn't catch that bee yourself?'

'No.'

'And bringing it to school wasn't even your idea?'

'No, it was Auntie Parveen's,' replied Umer.

Without even noticing it, I had come to a stop. You could almost hear the cogs in my brain crunching as they processed this new bit of information. Clunk-crunch-CLICK!

'She knew . . .' I gasped.

'Huh?' said Umer, clearly confused.

'She knew about Miss Crumble's allergy when she gave you that bee. She must have!'

'What? You think Auntie Parveen knew Miss Crumble would have an allergic reaction? Don't be daft – it's just a coincidence.'

Maybe Umer was right. Maybe I was being daft. Maybe it *was* all just a coincidence. But something in me was screaming otherwise. All these missing teachers – could the aunties be behind it? Could they be arranging every one of these accidents and injuries, just to take volunteer jobs at the school? It didn't make any sense.

And then, for the first time in days, I thought of Grandpa. I remembered what he'd said about Auntie Uzma. About how convinced he'd been that something wasn't right.

All of a sudden I was certain. Grandpa was on to something. These aunties were up to no good.

'Grandpa!' I shouted as I burst through the front door at his place. 'It's me! Come out from wherever you're hiding. We gotta talk!'

A moment later Grandpa's head appeared at the top of the stairs, leaning out from round the corner.

David Chesterton's face popped into view a few feet below.

'I'm so sorry I didn't believe you,' I told him. 'You were right – there *is* something going on.'

He stared at me a moment.

'Come,' he said, then disappeared back round the corner, followed closely by his cat.

I found them up in the loft, in the same spot as last time.

'Damn, you've been busy,' I said, looking around.

And he had been. All the cardboard boxes had been rearranged to create a room full of weird boxy furniture. There was a cardboard armchair for sitting in, a cardboard sofa for stretching out on and a cardboard table for working at.

Most striking of all though was the wall. Taller than me, taller than Grandpa even, stood a wall of boxes, right up to the ceiling. On it, Grandpa had pinned all kinds of photos, drawings, maps and bits of paper. Pieces of red string connected one photo to another, joined sheets of paper to scribbled Post-it notes. It was a spiderweb of auntie-based observations.

Under other circumstances, seeing all this lot would have definitely left me thinking Grandpa had finally gone nuts. But recent events at the school had convinced me otherwise. The aunties were planning something. I was glad to have Grandpa on side.

'Whoa ...' I said, taking it all in. 'What *is* all this?'

'Investigation,' replied Grandpa.

'Investigation? This is some pretty professional-looking detective work, Grandpa. How'd you learn how to do this?'

Grandpa stared at me a moment. He looked like he was about to say something, but then changed his mind.

'Come,' he said, turning to the board, 'See. See.'

He gestured to a grainy photo of Auntie Uzma at the supermarket. It looked like it had been taken from inside a bush. She didn't seem like she was aware she was being photographed.

'You been snooping on Auntie Uzma?' I asked him.

'Mmm,' he said, nodding his head. 'And more, see?'

He gestured around the board. I noticed, for the first time, that not all of the photos were of Auntie Uzma. There were loads of different aunties up there.

'It ain't just her, is it?' I said. 'They're all acting weird.'

He nodded again.

'What's got into them?' I asked.

'Don't know,' he muttered. 'They go out late. Meet in supermarkets. Whisper . . .'

'You know, they've basically taken over the school?' I told him.

He nodded.

'All the teachers just keep vanishing,' I continued. 'They get sick or hurt, or accidentally stung by bees . . . Loads of different things that just look random. But it can't be random, because after they disappear, every single time, an auntie shows up and takes their place.'

'Where are teachers now?' he asked.

'Sick leave, most of 'em.'

'But where? Have you seen thcm?'

'What, like in the street? No. I don't know where they live.'

'OK, then we find them,' he said with a sharp little nod.

'Right, and then what?'

'When we find missing teachers, we find answers.'

And without another word, he turned and disappeared back down the hatch.

As we stepped out the front door, I noticed Grandpa had something wedged under his arm.

'What's that?' I asked him.

'Phone book,' he replied, pulling it out and riffling through the pages.

'Why'd we need a phone book?'

'Teachers' addresses.'

'Oh yeah, why didn't I think of that?'

'Old fool not so foolish, huh?' he said with a grin. 'Now, what are the teachers' full names?'

'Full name? You mean like their first name as well? How should I know? We just call them Mr So-and-so or Mrs Whatever.'

'You don't know Mrs Whatever's first name?' he asked, looking perplexed.

'Huh? Oh, right . . . no, there is no Mrs Whatever. It was just an example.'

'Oh,' said Grandpa. 'What about Mr So-and-so?'

'No, ignore those names – they ain't real. Point is, I don't know any teacher's first names. Or any second names when it comes to the dinner ladies. We just call them Moira and Betty and Ada. Stuff like that.'

'Hmm,' he said, coming to a stop at the end of the block, 'then this is useless,' he added, and he tossed the phone book into one of his neighbour's bins.

'Hold on,' I said, pulling the phone book back out of the bin and dusting it free of some rice. 'I might have an idea how we can get some names.'

'You remember?' he asked, looking hopeful.

'Nope, but I know someone who might . . .'

I'd not been round here for ages, so at first I wasn't sure I had the right house. But when I pressed the buzzer some kind of weird doorbell opera started to play. Definitely the right house. I heard a voice from the other side of the door.

'What are you doing here, Humza?' said Wendy Wang. 'I haven't finished working on the laptop yet.'

'I'm not here about the laptop. Open up and I'll explain.'

'I'm not allowed to open the door to strangers,' she replied.

'I ain't a stranger! I've known you since I was four!'

'Well, who's that behind you?'

'That's my uncle, Grandpa.'

There was a pause.

'Is he your uncle or your grandpa?' asked Wendy, sounding confused.

'He's my uncle. His name's Grandpa. Actually, his name's Tariq, but that doesn't matter. He's Auntie Uzma's husband. He wants to help us.'

There was silence for a moment. Then the door opened a crack and Wendy's hand slipped through, held out stiff, towards Grandpa.

'Nice to meet you,' said Wendy.

Grandpa shook Wendy's hand.

'Nice to meet you too,' he said.

The hand pulled back inside and the door swung open.

'I guess you can come in now,' said Wendy.

'Nah, that's OK,' I replied. 'We don't want to come in. I just need some of the missing teachers' names. You know any?'

'Their names? You mean their *full* names?'

'Exactly, so we can look 'em up in this,' I said, holding out the phone book.

'Um . . . I think I remember a few,' said Wendy, after a pause. 'Mr Pamplemousse is called Peter.'

'Peter Pamplemousse – great. Who else?'

'Um . . . Wanda Plum,' she added. 'She teaches

Year Threes.'

'Miss Plum. Perfect. Next?'

'Oh, there's Ada Whelp — she's a dinner lady. I think that's all I can remember off the top of my head. How many do you need?'

'That's probably enough to get started.'

Then a thought struck me.

'Hey, how about Mr Turnbull?' I asked her. 'Have you got his?'

'Mr Turnbull?' said Wendy, thinking hard. 'Sorry, no. I don't recall.'

'That's all right,' I told her, though I felt kinda gutted. 'Thanks for your help.'

'No problem,' she replied, with an awkward smile.

'I'll see you Monday, yeah?' I said, turning to walk back out the gate. 'Good luck with the laptop.'

'Goodbye, Wendy Wang,' said Grandpa, and we headed off in search of Peter Pamplemousse.

Year Five teacher Peter Pamplemousse lived over in Trum. Now if you ain't been to Trum (and, trust me, there's no point ever going to Trum), it's about a twenty-minute bus ride away from Eggington.

We found his house without too much trouble, but there was no sign of him anywhere — just a stack of post building up inside the door. According to his neighbour, Pamplemousse had just upped and vanished one day, with only a note to explain that he'd decided to go and live with his mother in Scotland. It looked like a dead end.

Next up was Wanda Plum. We had to get the number 28 back into town, then two more buses out to where she lived in Hogfurst Mallet. The sun was already pretty low in the sky by the time we rang the front doorbell. Once again, there was no answer.

'Another dead end,' I said, bending down to look through the letterbox.

Inside was the same big pile of post as we'd seen at Mr P's place.

'Who is next on list?' said Grandpa.

'We've only got one name left,' I replied. 'Ada Whelp.'

'OK,' said Grandpa, and he began flicking through the phone book to find her. 'Here we are. Ada Whelp, 28b Ocelot Mews, Ikingham.'

'Ikingham?' I said. 'We can't get to Ikingham – it's miles away. Damn it, I wish one of us could drive.'

'Another bus?' he suggested.

'Yeah, with, like, six changes. We wouldn't get back until midnight.'

'Maybe try telephone?' suggested Grandpa.

'Good idea!' I replied. 'Give me your phone.'

'What phone?' he said, looking blank.

'Ah, man! You ain't got a phone either? That means we have to go all the way home just to make a call!'

'Can we use a payphone?' he asked.

'If we can find one,' I said, 'but these days most of 'em are just used as public toilets.'

'They make them into toilets?' asked Grandpa, looking confused.

'Not officially,' I replied.

'Oh . . .' he said, wrinkling his nose up.

'But I'm pretty sure there's still one outside the library. We'd have to go back into town, but the bus would drop us just round the corner.'

'Good. We'll go there,' said Grandpa.

And without another word we set off to use the library payphone.

'Oh my . . .' said Grandpa, looking down at the mess that used to be a public phone box.

I don't know if he was more disappointed by the fact that it had clearly become a toilet over the last decade, or because someone had ripped out the receiver, leaving just a wire dangling in its place.

'The youth of today,' I said, shaking my head.

'I guess that is that?' said Grandpa.

I was about to agree with him when something through the window caught my eye.

'Not so fast . . . I got an idea.'

Inside the library, I paid a pound to the librarian for half an hour on the computer.

'I don't know what I was thinking!' I told Grandpa, as I typed. 'Why go all the way across town looking for teachers when we can just check 'em out online? Teachers can't help posting stuff about their social lives. They think we can't see it for some reason, but most of us know more about computers than they do.'

While I was typing, I'd opened one of the social network sites popular among teachers and created a profile for Grandpa. He looked surprised when I used the webcam to snap his photo.

'It's me,' he said with a grin, admiring his new profile pic.

'Yup,' I replied. 'You've officially joined the twenty-first century, Uncle.'

Three minutes later we were looking at the profile page for ageing dinner lady Ada Whelp. The most recent status update was from three days ago. It read:

Ada Whelp is on holiday

Underneath that was a photograph of Ada standing beside an enormous mountain, surrounded by cherry blossom. I know dinner ladies aren't meant to be photogenic, but, even so, it was a pretty terrible shot. She looked like she'd been dragged out of bed, through a bush and halfway up a mountain.

'Where is that? China?' I asked.

'Japan,' said Grandpa. 'Mount Fuji.'

'Man, I thought Ikingham was far. I ain't got a clue how many buses it'd take to get to Japan.'

Next I typed in 'Wanda Plum' and hit SEARCH. Her profile popped up immediately.

'Huh, that's weird,' I said. 'It looks like Miss Plum's on holiday too.' Her last post was from a few days back and featured a photo of Miss Plum in front of an enormous waterfall. She didn't seem that impressed to be there either.

'I thought long holidays were the only reason for becoming a teacher. She looks like she'd rather be in bed than wherever that is.'

'Niagara Falls,' said Grandpa, leaning in to scrutinize the photo.

Finally, we looked up Peter Pamplemousse. Same as the rest: one update, one photo, one sleepy-looking teacher in an exotic location.

'Man, what the hell? He's on holiday too! What's up with that?'

Grandpa didn't answer. He had a puzzled look on his face.

'I know this one though,' I said, pointing to the enormous orange gorge behind Mr Pamplemousse. 'That's the Grand Canyon, yeah?'

'Mmm,' agreed Grandpa, '. . . Grand Canyon.'

He sounded far away.

'What is it?' I asked him.

'Something . . . something is not right . . . But . . . what?'

I didn't have any answers. Our search had only raised more questions. Why were all the teachers on holiday now? Why could none of them take a half-decent photograph? And *why* would anyone pick a phone box for a toilet when it had glass walls? It was all a mystery.

We paid 30p for a printout of everyone's holiday snaps, to add to Grandpa's investigation board, then headed to the exit. It was dark when we got outside.

'Home time,' said Grandpa.

'What? No!' I replied. 'We can't go home yet. We've got to figure this out!'

'It will have to wait,' said Grandpa, putting a hand on my shoulder. 'People will wonder where we are. Get suspicious. They cannot find out we are on to them. All we know for sure is that these aunties are dangerous.'

We walked home in silence, trying to put together all the different pieces. None of it made sense. These teachers weren't just gone from the school. They'd completely vanished from their lives.

CHAPTER EIGHT
WEIRD WEEKEND

Now, with it being the weekend, I figured Grandpa and I were gonna have all the time we needed to get to the bottom of this thing. Yeah, right. Between Dad making me play cricket and Mum making me help prepare for Sunday's big family dinner, we didn't get *any* investigating done. Dad was ready to pounce before I'd even got out of bed.

'Cricket!' he shouted, leaning in through my door.

'Aargh!' I yelled, jumping in fright.

'We have a match today,' he added with a grin. 'Get dressed! We leave in four minutes.'

'Actually, I thought I might go look after Grandpa instead. He's . . . uh . . . he's been a bit off colour.'

'He is always off colour,' said my dad. 'It's hard to

tell if he is alive most days. We have almost buried him on six occasions.'

'Right, but I still think I should —' I began, but Dad cut me off.

'Today you are playing cricket!' he shouted. 'And you are going to win!'

'Can't I miss it, just this once, Dad?'

'If you disobey me, boy, I swear I will ship you straight to your uncle in Pakistan. I have already purchased a crate!'

'What? No you haven't.'

'You want me to fetch the crate?' he bellowed. 'I will fetch the crate! Don't make me fetch the crate!'

I bit my tongue. I could never be sure when he actually meant it or when he was just being mental. He used to tell me that I once had a brother who was so disobedient he'd packaged him up and sent him to live in Pakistan for eighty years. Was he lying? You tell me. I couldn't take the risk. The investigation was just going to have to wait.

An hour later we were standing with the rest of the cricket team in the middle of a playing field. The others looked as miserable to be there as I did.

'Hey, guys!' I said, forcing a smile. 'Ready for some cricket?'

'I hate cricket,' replied Jamal Jones, barely looking at me.

Wow, it takes a special coach to make Jamal Jones hate cricket. My dad had a gift.

The team we were meant to be playing seemed like normal happy kids. They were doing a few warm-ups, running back and forth, catching and hitting the ball. Our team just sat around in the shade, looking as tired as we were miserable. Even walking up from the car park had left us out of breath. And there were a lot more bellies on show than there used to be.

Maybe this wasn't a case of shrunken laundry after all. I looked down at my own belly, sticking out from under my top. Hmm, definitely bigger. And, I swear, Jamal had never had a tummy on him before now. There was no two ways about it: all of us had piled on the pounds since the aunties showed up. Could this be part of their plan?

'Mohammed Ali Khan!' came a voice from nearby.

My dad turned to see who was calling his name. His mouth fell open.

'Abdul Saeed Siddiki!' he gasped. 'My old nemesis!'

'I have never forgotten that day on Manora Beach,' he said, 'when you cheated and stole victory from me and my brothers at the tyre factory.'

'Cheated?' shouted my father. 'We won *despite* your cheating!'

'Ha!' laughed Siddiki. 'Well, today I will have my revenge. My team arc the greatest twelve-and-under cricket team this side of Lahore!'

'And mine,' replied my dad, 'are the greatest team of any age, anywhere on the planet!'

The other team burst out laughing. Even a few of our team smirked at the claim. What was he thinking? Next he'd be placing bets on us.

'One hundred pounds says we beat you like the wretched dogs you are!' shouted my dad.

'Wretched dogs'? Huh. I guess that's one way to refer to a bunch of pre-teens playing a cricket friendly.

'Why not make it interesting?' said Siddiki. 'Two hundred pounds!'

'Ha!' shouted my father. 'There is nothing interesting about two hundred pounds! Not when you have –' he started going through his wallet, then emptying the change out of his back pocket – 'two hundred and seven pounds, thirty-one pence, and a half-full loyalty card for Uzbek Fried Chicken!'

'Agreed!' roared Siddiki, whipping out his own loyalty card for Uzbek Fried Chicken. 'May we thrash you like a herd of escaped goats!'

'You are the goats who have escaped and will require thrashing!' said my dad, his eyes bulging from his head.

If our cricket was half as terrible as that comeback, this was still gonna be a disaster.

And it was.

The smell of burnt rubber filled the car. Dad was furious. I swear you could see a little bit of steam coming off his bald spot. To say it wasn't helping his driving would be an understatement.

'He cheated me!' shouted my father, skidding over a mini-roundabout. 'He cheated me and stole my money!'

'I don't think he did, Dad,' I replied, gripping on to the dashboard to keep myself from falling out of my seat. 'They beat us fair and square.'

'Impossible! No team of mine would ever lose to a cowardly dog like Siddiki!'

'But, Dad, haven't you noticed? We've all slowed down a bit . . .'

'He must have poisoned you then!' shouted my dad.

'I don't think so. I've been wondering if it's how much everyone's been eating. You know, since the aunties came to help at the school?'

'He probably put chemicals in the reservoir!' roared my dad, not listening to a word I was saying. 'Or some sort of gas in the air vents! Or sorcery! I would not put it past him to use sorcery.'

I could see there was no point discussing it with him while he was riled up. But I'd definitely be mentioning my theory to Grandpa when I saw him. Because, if I didn't know better, I'd swear the aunties had been fattening us up for something . . .

Next, it was Mum's turn to screw up my weekend. The whole of Sunday morning was wasted helping her get ready for family dinner that afternoon. It was kind of a tradition for us all to get together like this on a Sunday, all the aunts and uncles and cousins, eating and talking and catching up. But seriously, man, did I really have to help with the cooking? Apparently, the answer was yes.

The only good thing was knowing that Grandpa

would definitely be there. I'd been desperate to talk to him again since our investigation had begun. And I knew I was on to something with the food. I just knew it.

We drove over to Auntie Salma and Uncle Bashir's place a little before five. The car boot was full of the rattling dishes we'd spent the morning preparing. Mum insisted on driving so Dad didn't wreck all our hard work. Dad was still in a foul mood about yesterday's cricket, so he just sat sulking in the passenger seat, not saying a word.

When we arrived, I followed them up the path to the front door, carrying a big bowl of butter chicken. My mum had cooked a lot, but nothing out of the ordinary. It's like this most weeks. Everyone shows up, everyone cooks, everyone stuffs their faces. Whatever was going on with the aunties, my mum didn't seem to be in on it. Auntie Salma, on the other hand, I wasn't too sure about . . .

'*Hiii-eeeee!*' squealed Auntie Salma as she tore open the door.

She pushed between my parents, nearly knocking their plates to the floor, and grabbed me by the cheeks with both hands. She squeezed them with her super-strong auntie fingers, giggling like a crazy person. With my arms full of butter chicken, I couldn't even defend myself. I was helpless.

'Get off, Auntie!' I said, shaking my head, but it was no good. She had me in her death grip.

'Beautiful fat boy!' she said, laughing. 'Come in, come in, come in!'

She took the bowl of butter chicken out of my hands, before bumping my dad out of the way and hurrying back inside. I was just about to follow everyone in when I heard a hiss from the bushes.

'*Psssst!*' said the voice.

I looked over to find Grandpa squatting in a hedge, his face peering out at me like some limited-edition Asian gnome.

'All right, Grandpa? What you doing in a hedge?'

'Aunties,' he replied. '*So* many aunties.'

'Oh right . . . So you're just going to hang out in the bush then?'

'I was waiting for you,' he said.

'Doesn't Auntie Uzma think it's kind of weird that you're sitting outside in a shrub?'

'She does not care. As long as I don't get in the way of her cooking, she doesn't seem to notice what I do.'

'I knew it!' I said. 'It *is* the food! There's something going on with all this cooking. At first I thought it was just a nice change, all the delicious food at school, but they're up to something.'

'Up to what?' asked Grandpa.

'Fattening us up to eat us!' I said as dramatically as I could.

'Hmm, maybe,' replied Grandpa, not sounding convinced. 'Maybe not.'

'Why? It makes sense, doesn't it? Aunties are pretty weird and sinister anyway, so it wouldn't take a lot for them to turn fully evil. And kids have got to be tastier than adults – like how lamb's tastier than dirty old sheep. They probably just went crazy and decided it was time they ate all the kids.'

'I don't know,' said Grandpa. 'It does seem a lot of work just to eat some children.'

'Mmm,' I said, thinking it through. 'I guess getting rid of all those teachers and taking their jobs *is* quite a lot of trouble to go to. Maybe there is more to the plan . . . But what?'

'That is what we must find out,' he said, leaping up from his bush and nearly falling flat on his face in the process.

I took him by the elbow and helped him on to the path. It was time to face the aunties.

There were four of them at dinner that day (five if you count Mum). Each auntie wearing a different-coloured shalwar kameez. Each was surrounded by a half-dozen steaming dishes. Each was forcing food on everyone around them. But how could we know who was in on it and who wasn't? How could we tell who was a proper auntie and who was an evil auntie?

All my little cousins were running around playing as usual. They obviously didn't suspect a thing. Grandpa and I were sitting together at one end of the table, watching everyone. Dad was at the far side of the room, between Uncle Bashir and Uncle Rabi, though he wasn't talking to either of them. Instead he was just slumped there sulking, occasionally muttering something about that coach Siddiki guy under his breath. The uncles just ignored it, talking across him like he wasn't there.

'Whatcha reckon, Grandpa?' I whispered.

'Hard to say,' he whispered back. 'Pretty normal so far. Except for all these fat cousins.'

He was right. These kids were ballooning. It had only been two weeks or so since I'd last seen them, but they'd all put on at least a stone. The adults weren't doing much better. Uncle Rabi had a triple chin where his double chin used to be, and was having to use an extension cord as a belt. But that wasn't going to stop the aunties. They kept right on serving dish after dish after dish . . .

Eventually, Mum started to politely refuse – which is never easy at an auntie house, even for another auntie. This time, though, the response was crazy. At first, one auntie flocked to her with a dish. Then, seconds later, another one. Still Mum refused their offers.

Soon there were three of them, each offering my mum something different, each pushing her to have one more bite, just one more . . . In under a minute all four aunties had surrounded my mum and were holding out spoons of curry and daal and kheer.

'No, really, I am so very full,' begged Mum, but they wouldn't listen.

Eventually she gave in and took another bite, nodding and smiling as she struggled to swallow it. But would they leave her alone? Yeah, right.

'Oh, go on,' said Auntie Uzma, waving her spoon of biryani, 'you are just skin and bones, Nausheen!'

'Yes,' said Auntie Salma, 'have a little laddoo.'

'Eat, eat, eat,' said Auntie Noor, waggling a pakora under Mum's nose.

'This is mental,' I said to Grandpa. 'Look at them. They're obsessed with her.'

'Hmm,' he said with a nod and a grim little frown. 'She is an auntie also. They won't stop until it is done.'

It took me a moment to realize what he was saying.

'You mean . . . they want her to join them . . .' I gasped.

Grandpa put his hand on my shoulder but didn't say anything more.

This must be how they went about it. Recruiting. It had something to do with the food. But what?

How does force-feeding someone turn them evil? None of it made sense.

I had a bad feeling as I walked into school on Monday morning. The whole place seemed sinister now. Everywhere you looked there was a smiling, cuddly, colourful auntie. Every room you entered had a plate of food, or a bowl of sweets laid out, ready to be snacked on. Delicious, mouth-watering smells had replaced the familiar old stink of the place.

I found Umer sitting at his usual desk, reading the back of a bag of crisps.

'Why you reading that packet of crisps?' I asked him as I sat down.

'It's today's assignment,' he replied. 'Read something delicious, then eat as much of it as you can.'

I snatched the bag of crisps from him and threw it out the window.

'Hey!' he said, looking offended. 'Why'd you do that?'

'It's the food!' I whispered. 'They're up to something with all the food.'

Umer looked about the room. There were kids reading sweet packets, ice-cream tubs, fizzy drinks.

Kids chomping away on all the most delicious, sugary food you could find in the supermarket. They all looked pretty happy – except for Wendy Wang, who was staring irritably at an apple.

'Did you not understand the assignment, Wendy?' asked Auntie Uzma from the front of the room.

'No,' replied Wendy, sounding as annoyed as she looked. 'I do not understand why we would waste our time with this.'

'That is because you have brought in the wrong type of food,' said Auntie Uzma, smiling. 'You were meant to bring in your favourite delicious treat.'

'I like apples,' said Wendy, not budging.

'But there is nothing to read on an apple but a tiny little plastic sticker,' replied Auntie Uzma, looking confused. 'The best sugary, fatty, delicious foods have all sorts of tasty ingredients and additives to read. And, when you're done with that, you can treat yourself by eating it!'

'I'll stick with my apple,' said Wendy, staring hard at Auntie Uzma.

Auntie Uzma stared right back at her, the smile slipping from her face.

'I think perhaps you are wanting to spend

another day with the headmaster, Wendy Wang?'

'Suits me fine,' replied Wendy, shoving her chair back and storming out of the room.

Wow, what had happened to this place? Everything was upside down. Wendy was an angry rebel, I was captain of the cricket team and Umer was a hardworking student. I looked over at him and he was reading another bag of crisps.

'Damn it, man, where'd that come from?' I snapped.

'I brought a family pack,' he replied.

'Give me that,' I said, grabbing the second bag of crisps and chucking it out the window.

'Ah, come on, Humza!' he moaned. 'I'm hungry.'

'What did I just say about doing what these aunties tell you? It's dangerous!'

'I thought you were happy about all the food,' said Umer, looking confused.

'I was, but can't you see? It's all connected! The missing teachers, the aunties, everyone putting on weight? It's all part of their plan.'

'What plan?' asked Umer.

'I don't know. I'm still working that out,' I replied, sounding as frustrated as I felt.

For the rest of the lesson, I did my best

to explain to Umer about my and Grandpa's investigation. I told him about how we'd tried to track down the missing teachers and come up empty-handed. About dinner with the aunties and how weird it had been. I told him about David Chesterton hissing at Auntie Uzma, and the weird auntie meetings Grandpa had observed at the 24-hour supermarket.

Umer sat and listened to everything. He seemed to be following it all – though I did have to chuck two more bags of crisps out the window when he got hungry.

When the lesson was over, we headed straight to Mr Offalbox's office to look for Wendy Wang. She was sitting in the corner reading a book. Mr Offalbox was nowhere to be seen.

'*Psst! Wendy*,' I whispered from the door.

She looked up at us.

'Oh, hey,' she said. 'You'd better not stay. He'll be back in a minute.'

'How'd it go with the laptop? Did you crack it?' I asked.

Wendy nodded. 'I got in, but there were no clues. Nothing about the teacher absences or all the aunties. Just a normal computer.'

'Damn. That's a shame,' I replied. 'I thought you might be on to something there.'

'Here you go,' said Wendy, reaching into her bag. 'I've deactivated the password. Do what you want with it, I guess. Doesn't really matter any more.'

Wendy sounded more depressed than I'd ever known her. I was just about to reach over and take the laptop, when a shadow fell across the room. We didn't have to turn round to know who it was. Wendy shoved the computer back into her bag.

'What are you boys doing in my office?' demanded Mr Offalbox.

'Uh . . . well . . .' I replied. 'Would you believe me if I said we were helping Wendy with her homework?'

'No,' growled Mr Offalbox. 'I would not.'

'Oh, right,' I replied. 'Well, give me a minute and I'll come up with something else.'

'Get outside now or the three of you will be in detention for the rest of the week!' shouted Mr Offalbox.

'You don't need to tell me twice,' I said with a smile. 'Later, OK, Wendy?'

Wendy nodded, patting the laptop-shaped bulge in her bag. We were out of there faster than you could say 'five-day-detention'.

At quarter to four, we were at the school gates, waiting for Wendy to finally be released. They had to let her go sooner or later, right? Whatever the case, I was gonna be real late for getting to Grandpa's today. Umer's stomach was rumbling and he didn't look happy at all.

'When can I have something to eat, Humza?' he begged.

'You can eat whenever you want, man, but don't let them pull the wool over your eyes. They're feeding you up for something.'

He grumbled quietly to himself for a moment, until he was interrupted by a loud beeping that seemed to be coming from somewhere between us. We both looked around.

'What was that?' asked Umer.

'I dunno,' I replied. 'Sounds kinda familiar though.'

A moment later it beeped again. It was coming from my bag. Then it hit me. I knew what it was!

'My pager!' I shouted.

I couldn't remember the last time anyone had bothered paging me. I pulled the little black box from my bag and opened the message:

WHERE ARE YOU? WHY AREN'T YOU HERE? CALL NOW! URGENT! GRANDPA

'Quick, I need to borrow your phone,' I said to Umer. 'Something's up with Grandpa.'

'Sure,' replied Umer, fishing his crusty old mobile out of his bag and handing it over.

'Hello?' came Grandpa's voice.

'It's me – what's going on?'

'Where are you? You have to get here, now!' he said, sounding kinda scary.

'I'm still at school. I'll be there soon though.'

'No. Right now!' he snapped. 'I have something.'

'What is it?'

'I found them!'

'Who? The teachers? Where are they?'

'Mount Fuji, Niagara, Grand Canyon – I found the link!'

'The link? What is it?' I asked.

But there was no answer. Everything was quiet.

'Grandpa?' I called out.

I could hear him breathing. Short, sharp gasps. He was trying to keep quiet. Someone else must be there.

'Grandpa?' I whispered. 'What's going on?'

170

For a moment even his breathing stopped.

Silence . . .

Then, with a crashing that shook the other end of the line, I heard him yell.

'Oh no!' cried Grandpa, his voice full of fear.

'Grandpa?' I called.

'You!' he shouted. 'What have you done with my wife? No! Stop . . .'

Click . . . The line went dead.

'What is it?' asked Umer, looking afraid.

'I gotta go,' I said, pushing his phone against his chest. 'I gotta get to Grandpa's!'

And, with that, I ran out of the school as fast as I'd ever run.

CHAPTER NINE
ACCESS DENIED

I was gasping for breath by the time I skidded to a stop at Grandpa's front door. My hands were shaking as I slid the key into the lock. But, when I went to turn it, it wouldn't budge. I twisted harder, double-checked that I had the right key – it was no good. I couldn't get in.

I rang the bell and banged on the door with my fists. No answer.

'Grandpa! It's me! I'm here!' I shouted through the letterbox.

That's when I saw something inside moving towards me. But it definitely wasn't Grandpa. It was much too big. The door swung open.

'*Hiii-eeeee!*' said Auntie Uzma like nothing at all was wrong.

'Where's Grandpa? Why doesn't my key work?

Why are you back so early?' I blurted it out all at once, still gasping for breath.

'Don't you worry, Humza,' said Auntie Uzma with a weird smile. 'Your uncle is going to be just fine. But he has overdone it lately with all his outings and now he must rest.'

'He seemed fine,' I replied. 'Actually, he was more alive than I'd ever seen him.'

'Well, you have obviously tired him out then. What have you two been up to exactly?' she asked, her eyes narrowing with suspicion.

'Uh, nothing. Magic tricks mainly,' I answered as fast as I could.

'Well, there will be no more of that. He needs to rest, so you must go home. Here . . .' she said, and reached over to a table by the door to pick up a large plate of sweet, sticky jalebis. 'For your mother. Tell her she has to eat it all. She is still so skinny!'

I accepted the plate of fried treats and backed away from the door. There was no sign of Grandpa in any of the windows. No sign of anything out of the ordinary – unless you count Auntie Uzma's eerie grin as she stood in the hall watching me. What the hell was going on? What had she done with Grandpa? Why would she change the locks?

I dumped the plate of jalebis in a skip round the corner and ran home. There was no way I was gonna help those aunties fatten up my mum.

I was already shouting before I'd got through the front door.

'Mum! Where are you?'

There was no answer. I ran through the house, yelling, but there was no sign of her. I figured she must have gone out and I was about to give up when I spotted her from the bedroom window. She was down in the garden, on her hands and knees, beside a big pile of weeds.

I pulled open the window and yelled down to her. 'We need to stop Auntie Uzma! We need to stop all the aunties!'

She looked startled and clearly had no idea where the voice was coming from.

'Up here!' I shouted.

Mum looked up at me, holding a muddy trowel up to shade her eyes.

'Stop shouting! The whole neighbourhood will hear you,' she said.

'Good! They need to hear this. There's something going on, Mum. The aunties are up to something.'

'Oh, for goodness' sake, Humza!' said Mum, shaking her head. 'If this is your way of getting out of helping Grandpa, it's not going to work.'

'What are you talking about? I'm trying to help Grandpa! That's what I'm telling you! He needs help!'

'Sounds like the boy wants to weasel out of it,' came a voice from above my head. 'He tried to do the same with cricket!'

Craning out the window, I looked up to see my dad ten feet above me on the roof. He was on all fours, with a big fistful of gutter sludge in each hand.

'Dad, you gotta listen to me,' I said. 'Grandpa's been kidnapped by Auntie Uzma, and we have to rescue him so we can stop the aunties taking over the world!'

My dad looked at my mum. She looked at him. They both looked at me. Then they burst out laughing.

They were still laughing when I pulled the window closed and sat down on the bed. They weren't going to listen. They would never believe me. I was going to have to get to the bottom of this myself.

The next day, for the first time ever, I was at school before anyone else. I parked myself by the gates and sat waiting for Wendy to arrive. I had to see her before she got thrown back into the headmaster's office. Kids started piling in before long; aunties too . . .

I was just starting to think that maybe there were no original staff members left in the place, when I saw Mr Offalbox pull up in his funny little car. I say 'car' – it was more like a go-kart. It would have made a perfectly good five-seater for a normal family, but with Offalbox behind the wheel it looked like an ape had nicked a dodgem. He had to take the top down just to get in. Anyone in the back seat would have been crushed to death in minutes. Thank God he didn't have kids of his own back there.

'Humza,' he said, as he passed. 'Up to no good, I presume?'

'I'm waiting to see Wendy Wang,' I replied. 'She keeps getting in trouble and it ain't fair.'

'If it wasn't fair, she wouldn't be sent to my office,' replied Mr Offalbox. 'Though I admit it was a little unexpected to begin with.'

'It's these aunties, man!' I cried. 'They ain't right!'

'Aunties?' he said, laughing. 'What, you mean the volunteers? Come on, Humza. You can't blame *them* for your troubles. I tell you, without their help during this staff crisis, the school would have had to close down.'

'That doesn't sound so bad to me.'

'One day, Humza, you'll thank me for your education.' He smiled.

'Yeah, if I live that long,' I replied.

Mr Offalbox looked genuinely perplexed at this.

'Just you behave yourself,' he said, then turned and headed inside.

It was almost time for the final bell to go, when Wendy appeared at the top of the road. She was trudging in like she really didn't want to be there.

'Hurry up, Wendy!' I shouted.

She raised her head and gave a small wave when she spotted me.

'Hey, Humza,' she said when she got closer. 'I suppose you're after this?'

She pulled the laptop out of her bag and handed it to me.

'Thanks,' I said, slipping it into my own backpack. 'But I actually wanted to talk to you as well. You look terrible.'

'I hate this place,' she replied, looking like she might cry. 'They've ruined everything.'

'I agree,' I said, 'and I *always* kind of hated it.'

I looked around the playground. It was completely deserted. Classes would have started by now. When I felt safe we were alone, I took a step towards Wendy and lowered my voice.

'Listen, I'm one hundred per cent positive there's something going on with Auntie Uzma,' I told her. 'She's acting super weird now. She won't let me see Grandpa – she's even changed the locks.'

'Why?' asked Wendy. 'What happened?'

'I don't know. Grandpa found something. Something important to do with their plan.

They're fattening us up for something. I've just got no idea what.'

'I guess it doesn't matter. Without any proof, who's going to listen?' she said. She looked really beaten down. Even the anger from yesterday had gone out of her.

'Well, that's why we're gonna get some proof,' I replied. 'That's what Grandpa and I were working on before he disappeared. He said he found something to do with the missing teachers. Something about them being on holiday. He tried to tell me, but the line went dead.'

'Maybe he left a clue somewhere?' said Wendy.

'Exactly! That's what I thought. But now I can't even get into his house to look.'

'I don't see what we can do then. The aunties have got all the power. Everyone thinks they're heroes for keeping the school open. We're just kids. No one listens to us.'

'Come on, Wendy – we'll get to the bottom of this,' I said, putting my hand on her shoulder. 'We have to.'

School that morning was weird. Super weird. On the surface it was the same as it had been the last couple of weeks. Auntie Uzma was doing her usual thing: loads of food, not much learning. But it was different now somehow. I couldn't help but feel she was watching me. Maybe I was being paranoid, but you would be too with everything I had going on.

We were in the middle of a spelling game where each kid had to stand up and spell a word in front of the class. If you got your word right you got a cake. And if you got your word wrong you got a slightly different cake. I was in line behind Jemima Tunk, who was called up to spell the word 'delicious'.

'Delicious,' said Jemima. 'D–E–L–I . . . uh . . . S–H–O–U–S. Delicious.'

'Oh, so close, Jemima!' said Auntie Uzma. 'I tell you what, because you were so nearly there, you can have a right cake *and* a wrong cake. How does that sound?'

'Thanks,' said Jemima, greedily accepting both cakes.

Man, it was a miracle no one had popped yet. We must have been getting through ten meals a day. Every kid in the room had a tummy now. Umer was working on his third chin.

They'd have to start reinforcing the walls soon, to stop the school collapsing.

'OK, Humza, you're next,' said Auntie Uzma. 'Your word is "caution".'

'"Caution"?' I replied. 'Like being careful?'

'That's right,' said Auntie Uzma. 'As in: "to avoid danger, you must show great caution."'

She was looking right at me, with that weird smile – sweet and threatening all at once. I didn't know if everyone else could see it, but Wendy definitely could. She looked worried.

'Why'd I get that word?' I asked. 'Everyone else had words like "doughnut" and "fudge".'

'They're just random words from a list, Humza. Nothing to do with you. Now hurry up and spell "caution".'

It looked like I didn't have much of a choice. I had to play along.

'Caution,' I said. 'K–O–R–S–H–U–N. Caution.'

'Oh, that'll do,' said Auntie Uzma, and she handed me a cake.

I took it from her and went back to my seat. There was no way I was going to eat it. When she wasn't looking, I wrapped it up in a napkin and shoved it into my bag. My hand hit something hard. The laptop! I'd already forgotten it was there. Just seeing it made me smile. I thought of Mr Turnbull and all the work we'd put in. I remembered how close we were to getting the track finished and how good it all sounded. I just wished things could go back to how they were.

'Can I go to the toilet, miss?' I said.

'Of course you can,' she replied, 'and call me Auntie.'

Yeah, I thought, as I stood up, *but maybe you ain't my auntie after all*. Grabbing my bag, I walked out the door as Umer was stumbling his way through the word 'potato'.

I decided to do the only thing I could think of that might cheer me up. I took Mr T's laptop to the library, where I knew I could get a bit of peace and quiet, and I sat down in a corner where no one would be able see me. I put on my headphones as the computer loaded up. The audio software was already open, ready to go. There was the track, just as we'd left it; dozens of coloured little boxes stretched out along a two-minute timeline.

I was just about to hit PLAY when I saw her – Mrs Farooqi, the replacement librarian. You know the routine by now: brightly coloured dress, big weird smile, round as a wrecking ball – classic auntie. She was putting cupcakes out around the room for any kid who happened to wander in.

By leaning forward a little and looking through the gap in the bookshelf I could keep an eye on her while remaining out of sight. I figured I might as well get on with listening to the track. If I got caught it's not like things could get any worse . . . I hit PLAY.

The beat came in first. Ah, man, it was good. And that bass. I still couldn't figure it out. So deep. Exploding out and rushing in all at once. I loved it. Then my vocal kicked in. You know what? It wasn't too bad. Even my performance sounded better than I remembered. I smiled to myself. Felt a little pang of happiness. It wouldn't last . . .

'Ow,' I said, as a book hit me on the head.

I looked up to find the whole shelf was shaking. What was going on? I craned my head up to see over the books and into the next row, and there she was, Mrs Farooqi, right up against the other side of the bookshelf just ten feet away. She was leaning over like she was in pain or having some kind of seizure. I was about to jump up and check she was OK, when things got weird.

She was making this noise, a kind of groaning sound, coming from deep inside her. She turned in my direction and, for a second, I thought she might see me. But I was tucked far enough back in the shadows. She couldn't see a thing. I was safe. Or at least I thought I was.

Because that's when everything changed. Forever . . .

Mrs Farooqi opened her mouth wide. Too wide. Unnaturally wide.

And there it was. Inside her enormous mouth was wedged a great, fat white eyeball. It was staring out into the room, crammed in there between her teeth. It had to be the size of a tennis ball. It was pulsing with veins and had a large black pupil at its centre.

She began to retch, like a cat with a hairball. And every time she did, more and more of the creature began to slip free. A bulging bag of green, slug-like flesh followed the eye out of Mrs Farooqi's mouth. What the hell was this thing?

I fell backwards against the wall. I didn't know what I was looking at, but I knew I needed to get out of there fast. I jumped to my feet and pulled off my headphones. It took me a second to

realize it, but I could still hear the track playing.
'What the . . . ?'

That was when I noticed it: I'd never plugged
the headphones in. I must have been playing the
track aloud this whole time. How stupid could I
be? Blaring away in the corner like that, it was a
miracle I hadn't been caught.

Mrs Farooqi was on her knees now, and at least
half a metre of the fat, slimy green slug monster
had spilled out on to the floor. Its big ugly eye was

looking about in wild panic. It had rows of little stubby green tentacles, running the length of its body. If that thing got free and caught me, who knew what it might do? I had to move fast.

If I went via the reference books and out past early readers, I could stay behind Mrs Farooqi and, with a bit of luck, avoid being seen by the monster. I slammed the laptop shut, scooped it into my bag and ran. But as soon as I did, she stopped shaking. The retching noise ceased and the green creature began to disappear back into her mouth. I didn't have long.

I was still behind her as Mrs Farooqi began to pull herself to her feet. If she turned round now, I was done for. But, instead, she began to straighten her hair and adjust her dress. I didn't pause for a second. I dived for the open door and out into the hallway. I ran without looking back.

I was dripping with sweat when I sat back down beside Umer. He knew something was up immediately. So did Wendy. They were both staring at me, wide-eyed.

'What's going on, Humza?' asked Umer, sounding nervous.

'I . . . it . . . she . . .' I mumbled.

I just couldn't find the words. I was in shock. Thankfully, it was nearly break time, because I couldn't get out of there fast enough. As soon as Auntie Uzma said we could go, I was out the door like a shot. Umer and Wendy had to run to keep up.

'What happened, Humza?' said Wendy when we got to the benches on the far side of the playground.

'She's a . . .' I started. 'There's a . . . it came out of her mouth,' I said, still struggling to think straight.

'What came out of whose mouth?' said Wendy.

'The librarian, the auntie, Mrs Farooqi,' I said. 'She's got a creature inside her.'

'A creature?' said Umer. 'What kind of creature?'

'I don't know, man. I ain't never seen anything like that before. It was big, and long, and green all over!'

'Like an alligator?' said Umer.

'No.' I shook my head. 'It looked like a slug.'

'So a slug then?' said Wendy.

'No, it was huge! It had one massive eyeball. It was covered with tentacles.'

They both stared at me for a moment.

'Like an emu?' said Umer.

'What? No! Do you know what an emu is?' I shouted.

Umer shook his head.

'Look, I don't know what the hell that thing was, but it wasn't like anything I've ever seen before, and I've watched both series of *Planet Earth*!'

'So you're saying it wasn't from Earth then?' asked Wendy.

She was looking at me like I might have gone mad.

'I know how it sounds, but I swear that's what I saw. There's a monster living in Mrs Farooqi!'

I knew that look they were giving me. I'd seen it before, far too often.

'I'm not lying, guys! You've got to believe me!'

'I don't know, Humza,' said Umer, frowning. 'Remember when you told me Mr Dawbry was a werewolf? I couldn't come in for a month after that. My parents made me talk to a doctor.'

'This ain't like that!' I yelled. 'I'm not making it up!'

'You told *me* the caretaker was a thousand years old and stayed young by eating children,' added Wendy.

'I admit it – I had bad intel on that one. But I'm

telling you I ain't wrong about this. I know what I saw. And if she's one of those things, then I bet you – the rest are too.'

'The rest? You mean the aunties? You think *this* is why they're acting weird?' asked Umer.

'Yeah, I do! It makes sense, doesn't it? I bet you they've all got one of these slugs in 'em.'

'Well, why haven't we seen one before?' asked Wendy. 'Why just this one time? Why right now?'

'I don't know. Maybe it was cos she didn't know I was there? I was hiding behind one of the bookshelves.'

They were both quiet for a time. They were still giving me that look.

'I don't know, Humza,' said Wendy. 'I want to believe you, but this is just the kind of thing you lie about.'

'You believe me, don't you, Umer?'

He had this anxious little frown on his face. I'd never seen him so conflicted.

'I . . .' said Umer, 'I mean . . . I want to . . .'

'Ah, man! I swear! On my dad's life! Hell, even on my mum's life! I ain't lying!'

'What *exactly* was going on when all this happened?' asked Wendy.

Her tone had changed a little. I could tell I was getting to her. She was starting to listen.

'Right,' I began. 'So I was hiding in a corner of the library so that I could play the track in peace. Farooqi was on the other side of the room, doing whatever she was doing. Putting out cupcakes or something.'

Wendy and Umer listened intently.

'I had just put on my headphones and hit PLAY, when she started freaking out. She was falling all over the place, knocking books off the shelves, making these weird noises. And then she starts coughing it up – this massive weird creature.'

'How did you get away?' asked Umer.

'I ran round the side and out the door. Just in time as well, cos that thing started going back into her mouth. Last thing I saw, she had stood up like nothing had even happened.'

'So it all just stopped?' said Wendy.

'Yeah, as quick as it had started,' I replied.

'There's nothing else you remember?' asked Wendy. 'It doesn't matter how small.'

'Oh yeah!' I blurted out. 'I was seriously lucky not to get caught. See, it turned out I'd forgotten to plug in my headphones the whole time. I hadn't even noticed. I'd been playing the track out loud.'

'Out loud?' said Wendy.

'Yeah, it must have been blaring.'

'And all this, the whole reaction, it happened during the time the track was playing?' asked Wendy, looking real intense all of a sudden.

'Uh . . . yeah, I guess,' I replied.

'The track . . .' she gasped. 'The track did it.'

'Did what?' asked Umer.

'The track caused the reaction,' said Wendy. 'It affected the creature somehow. Made it reveal itself.'

'You reckon?' I asked. 'Why would that happen?'

'I don't know yet,' replied Wendy. 'But it can't be a coincidence. Maybe something in the frequency of the audio affects them?'

'You mean they're allergic to Humza's music?' asked Umer, smiling a little.

'If you like,' replied Wendy.

'Shut up, man. No they ain't,' I snapped. 'It probably just came out so it could hear better.'

'Whatever the reason,' continued Wendy, 'it means we can prove it now – prove there's something going on.'

'Great! Then that's what we're gonna do!' I said. 'And it's gotta be in front of as many people as possible. Then they'll have to believe us.'

'We can play it through the loudspeakers in the hall,' said Wendy.

'Exactly!' I shouted. 'We just need a reason to get all the aunties together at once.'

'What about the talent show?' said Umer. 'That's coming up?'

'That ain't soon enough. We need to do this now,' I replied.

'Assembly?' suggested Wendy. 'We've got one tomorrow morning. I could get the laptop hooked into the speakers this afternoon without much trouble.'

'Perfect,' I replied. 'And I bet I could convince them to let us play the track. Tell 'em it's a song about eating contests or something. They'd go for that.'

'But tomorrow morning . . .' said Umer, 'is that going to be enough time?'

'It'll have to be,' I said. 'We need to get started right away. Wendy, you go see if you can get this hooked up to the sound system.'

I handed her the laptop.

'Umer,' I continued, 'you and me are gonna convince them to let us play at tomorrow's assembly.'

'OK,' said Umer, looking a little nervous.

'Don't worry, man,' I said to him. 'Once that beat drops, those things are gonna start freaking out. They won't be able to do a thing to us. The whole school will know they're real. We'll have saved everyone!'

We were all smiling now. Suddenly we had a way out of this. We were gonna be heroes!

CHAPTER TEN
THE ASSEMBLY

Umer was right. We didn't have much time to get set up. While Wendy went to sort out the technical side of things, we ran off to sweet-talk Mrs Masood. If anyone would be able to give us a slot at assembly to sing about food, it was that crazy sitar player. And I was pretty sure the headmaster wouldn't stand in the way of us cutting her session short. We found her in the playground at lunch, handing out chocolate bananas.

'Hey, Mrs M,' I said to her, as we walked up. 'That was a pretty sick set you played at assembly the other day. You've totally inspired us!'

'Oh good,' said Mrs Masood. 'Would you like a chocolate-dipped banana?'

'Yeah, great!' I said with the most enthusiastic smile I could manage. 'In fact, I'll take two!'

'Oooh, lovely,' she said, dishing them out.

'Listen, I have a big favour to ask you, and only you can help me.'

'Oh,' she replied, 'what is that?'

'Like I say, we were inspired by your music and decided to write a song of our own. It's all about food and eating and . . . uh . . . voluntary weight gain. It's called "Fat and Happy".'

'Ooooh! "Fat and Happy"!' she replied. 'I like the sound of that!'

'Yeah, so we wondered if we could play it at tomorrow's assembly?'

'Play it? For the other students?' she asked. 'Well, I don't see why not. Yes, that will be very nice for everyone to hear. Especially when it has such a positive message about consumption.'

'Great! Thanks, miss!'

'Would you like a chocolate banana too?' she said to Umer with a big smile.

'No thanks,' he replied. 'Humza says I'm not allowed.'

'Ha ha!' I laughed loudly, elbowing Umer in the ribs. 'That was just a joke! Of course you're allowed. Take two! Take six! Mmm, chocolate, right?'

'Oh, right. Thanks,' said Umer, and he helped

himself to a couple of the chocolate bananas.

'All right, miss – we'd better go,' I said. 'Gotta get practising.'

'See you in the morning,' she said with a smile.

'Can't wait!' I replied, beaming back at her.

The smile fell straight off my face as soon as my back was turned. When we got round the corner I dumped my bananas in the bin, then did the same with Umer's.

'Hey!' he cried. 'I thought I could have as many as I wanted!'

'No, man! Nothing's changed. They're still trying to fatten you up. I was just taking them so we wouldn't arouse any suspicion.'

'Oh,' replied Umer, sounding glum. 'You could have let me finish the one I was eating.'

'You've had enough, man! Look at us!'

There was no denying it, we had piled on the pounds. And we weren't the only ones. Looking around, every damn kid in the playground was eating a sugary snack. Everyone looked tired and hot and out of breath. We were starting to look like cattle on a farm. This had to stop.

Tomorrow we were gonna end it once and for all.

I barely slept that night. I just sat there wide awake for hours, going over it in my head. When the track started, all the aunties would begin freaking out. All those slugs would start appearing and everyone – the students, the headmaster – would see them.

And once they'd all seen it people would *have* to believe us. They might not listen to me, but they couldn't ignore an entire school. We'd be heroes for saving the day. And I'd be the biggest hero of all because it was my track and I'd figured it out.

It must have been 3 a.m. when I eventually

drifted off. My dreams were filled with giant green slugs, mountains of food and a billion brightly coloured aunties, chasing me through the streets. I gotta say, it wasn't the best night's sleep I ever got. But waking up was even worse . . .

SLAM! went the door. I bolted up in time to see my dad putting on his seat belt and hammering down the accelerator. We shot off like a bullet.

'What the hell?' I yelled.

I looked down and found I was still wearing my pyjamas. The sun was barely up. I turned round to see the entire cricket team sitting in the school minivan behind me. They all looked exhausted, rubbing their eyes and yawning.

'What's going on, Dad?' I shouted. 'Why am I in the minivan?'

'Cricket match!' he shouted back, turning the wheel and screeching round a corner.

'I'm in my pyjamas, man! Why aren't I in bed?'

'You were asleep. Didn't have time to wake you.'

'Are you insane? This is an abduction!' I yelled.

'Nonsense. As my child, you are basically my property. Like a microwave or some towels.'

'You're mad! What about the rest of the team?

They don't want to be here either. We're meant to be at school!'

'Irrelevant. The headmaster has approved it.' He grinned. 'So now we get to have rematch with that worthless dog Siddiki!'

'Dad, I can't play cricket today. Not today. I need to be at school!'

'School can wait. Today you play cricket!'

'But I need to stop the aunties!'

'The aunties?' My dad laughed. 'This nonsense again?'

'They're monsters! They're taking over everything!'

'Oh, come on, boy,' replied Dad, chuckling. 'If you keep making up these tall tales, no one will ever believe a thing you say. You must always speak the truth, like me!'

Oh my god! This was terrible! Umer and Wendy would be waiting for me. I needed to get back there. Whatever these aunties were up to, it could all be over any moment. Who's to say they wouldn't finish us off today?

I was considering jumping out of the van at the next traffic light – but it turned out Dad wasn't stopping for traffic lights. He wasn't stopping for anything. I swear, we came *THIS* close to hitting a police horse. If the aunties didn't kill me, Dad definitely would.

Ten minutes later we were at yet another school, standing in front of the same team who'd thrashed us over the weekend. Their coach approached my dad with his belly stuck out and a big grin on his face. My dad squared up to him, his own belly thrust forward until the pair of them met, navel to navel.

'So, I see you have slithered from your hole like the legless goat you are!' said Abdul Saeed Siddiki.

'It is *you* that is the legless goat!' shouted my father, thrusting his stomach out so hard that coach Siddiki had to take a step back. 'I am here to prove that you only beat me by cheating!'

'Ha!' laughed Siddiki. 'We won because your boys are doughy and out of shape, because they have Pakistan's least qualified coach and because they show up dressed in pyjamas!'

He pointed at me when he said this. All the boys on his team began to laugh. Dad looked round at me.

'Why are you still wearing pyjamas?' he hissed.

'Cos you kidnapped me from my bed!' I yelled. 'I ain't got any other clothes!' I could barely believe I was having this conversation.

'Kit is in the van,' he growled. 'Go and change immediately!'

I turned and stormed back towards the van.

Before I even got there I knew what I was going to do. I glanced around briefly to make sure my dad wasn't watching. And then I ran.

I ran and ran and ran and ran and ran and ran and ran (and walked a bit cos I had a stitch) and ran and ran and ran!

★

I don't know how long I ran for, but, I can tell you for sure, I'd never run that far or that fast in my life. When I got to the school gates I nearly collapsed. I was pretty sure I was having at least two heart attacks. But it didn't mean I could stop – not yet. I had to make it to that assembly. I had to save the day. I had to be a hero!

I stumbled up the stairs and tumbled into the assembly hall. I could see Mrs Masood at the front of the room, playing a tone-deaf cover of 'Kabhi Khushi Kabhie Gham' on the sitar. Umer and Wendy were standing to one side looking anxious. When they saw me they waved frantically. I made my way over, slipping past a dozen aunties, who all gave me the same strange look.

'Where you been, man?' said Umer.

'I got kidnapped. Don't worry about it – I'm here now,' I replied, still catching my breath.

'Why are you in your pyjamas?' asked Wendy, looking me up and down.

'Don't worry about that either. It's a long, stupid story. Are we good to go?'

'Uh-huh,' said Wendy. 'The laptop's all hooked

up to the sound system.' She pointed at the laptop, which was sitting on a little table to one side of the stage. 'When you're ready Umer's going to hit PLAY and you can do your rap.'

'Yeah, cool. I'll just mime along.'

'What? No,' said Wendy. 'It's just an instrumental.'

'What do you mean, "an instrumental"?' I asked her.

'I cleared the old vocals so you could perform it properly,' said Wendy. 'I thought that's what you'd want . . . You kept saying your new lyrics were the proper ones. That's not a problem, is it?'

'Uh, no, course not. I'm a professional,' I replied. 'I just thought, you know, I figured, for simplicity and everything, you know, I just figured . . .'

'Are you OK, Humza?' asked Umer.

'Yeah, course I am!' I snapped. 'This is nothing to me. I'm gonna rinse this! If there's any music industry people in the crowd today, I'll probably get a record deal.'

'I think it's mainly aunties and children,' said Umer, looking confused.

'Whatever. Just don't worry about me. I ain't nervous. Not at all. Not even a bit. Is it hot in here?

It's hot in here, isn't it? Why's it so hot? Someone, open a window!'

'You're talking pretty fast, Humza,' said Wendy. 'Just take a breath.'

'You take a breath!' I told her, not entirely sure what I meant by it.

And then the clapping started. I think the audience were mainly just relieved that Mrs Masood had finally finished playing the sitar. But, damn, that clapping was loud.

'And now, boys and girls,' said Mrs Masood, standing up from her stool. 'We have a special treat. Humza and Umer from Year Six have written a lovely song for us about the joys of eating delicious food.'

She had that slightly crazy smile on her face that I was getting used to seeing in the aunties. I pictured the eyeball staring out of Mrs Farooqi's mouth and I shuddered.

'Now, to make it even more fun,' she continued, 'your teachers will be handing out cakes for every student. Please take one and pass it on.'

At this point the aunties started passing cakes down each of the rows of kids.

'Here you are, Humza,' Mrs Masood said, and handed me a microphone.

Umer took his place behind the laptop. Wendy gave me a serious little nod. 'Good luck,' she said.

I walked out on to the stage and turned to face the entire school. Man, there were a lot of them. I wasn't used to seeing it like this. Not from this side of the stage. Hundreds of faces just staring at me. Waiting for me. Watching me.

But it was fine. Whatever. I wasn't scared. This was probably just excitement I was feeling. It felt quite a lot like wanting to throw up. Once that bass kicked in, it'd be fine. Those monsters would come out and everyone would see 'em. Everyone would know they were real. I could see Mr Offalbox standing at the back of the room, looking right at me. He'd have to believe me after this. I just had to begin. Just had to do it.

I looked round at Umer. He nodded at me, then hit PLAY. Boom! The bass, the beat. It all kicked in. This was it – those aunties were done for.

I looked around the room. Man, there were a lot of people here. I could feel sweat running down my forehead. It was definitely hot in here. The kids were all looking at me. The aunties were all looking at me. Nothing was happening.

'*Humza*,' hissed Umer.

I glanced round at him. He looked a bit panicked.

'Do something!' he whispered loudly.

I realized we'd already passed the part of the song where my vocal was meant to come in. I'd missed it somehow. I'd just have to start. I'd just have to do something. Anything . . .

But I couldn't. The words weren't there. None of them. Not the old lyrics, not the new ones. Nothing. I couldn't remember a thing. How the hell was it meant to start?

'I . . .' I began to say, but couldn't get any further.

I turned to Wendy. She looked desperate.

'Come on!' she urged.

Then the first kid started to laugh. It was a Year Five named Benton. He cracked up and started slapping his thigh. Who the hell was *he* to laugh at me with a name like Benton? His mates went next, laughing and pointing. Then the kids around them. Soon it was the whole school. Even some of the aunties were giggling.

And still I couldn't say a word.

The bass was pounding away in my head. Why hadn't the slugs come out? Why hadn't the aunties been affected? Why hadn't it worked?

'Nice pyjamas!' came a shout from somewhere

in the room. A bigger laugh followed.

I could suddenly see myself, standing there, centre stage, dressed in Optimus Prime pyjamas, with my mouth hanging open like a trout. Someone started to boo. Who boos an eleven-year-old? Then a few more joined in. This was bad. This was as bad as it gets.

. . . Nope. Of course it wasn't.

'*BOY!*' came a shout so loud that the booing and the laughter stopped all at once. I looked to the side of the stage and there he was; my dad, *glowing* with anger. It takes a lot to make an Asian dad go totally red, but it seemed like I'd managed it. Uh-oh.

'You cost us the game, boy!' shouted my dad. 'You humiliated me in front of that swine Siddiki! *Again!*'

I looked around for an exit. He saw it in my eyes and began to storm towards me, arms outstretched. Mr Offalbox was coming the other way – whether to stop me from escaping or to stop my dad from killing me, I couldn't tell. Either way I was stuck. If I didn't move I'd end up crushed between the two of them.

There was still a chance. If I was quick I might just be able to duck behind Umer, slip past Dad and make it to the door before anyone could grab me. It was my only hope. I ran for it.

For a split second I thought I was safe. But I tell you, for a big old guy in skintight cricket gear, my dad was quick on his toes. He lurched towards me, grabbing for my pyjama collar. I ducked just in time. Umer dived to one side. My dad missed us by an inch. But he didn't miss the laptop. He caught it head-on.

The delicate piece of machinery was thrown straight up into the air. The music fell silent as the cord was yanked from its socket. Every eye in the place watched the laptop soar upwards, before following it back down. There wasn't a sound in the room when it hit the floor and exploded into a thousand pieces.

'*Noooo!*' I yelled, diving for it on my knees.

It was no good. The laptop was now just a smoking pile of plastic and metal. A hand grabbed my collar and yanked me to my feet. I didn't even resist.

'You are coming with me!' said my father, and he marched me from the hall.

The silence was deathly.

★

Now, I've been in trouble before. I'm a master at trouble. Getting into it, getting out of it, getting back into it again. You could say trouble's my middle name (it ain't – it's Mohammed – but, you know, if I had two middle names, Trouble would be one of them). And with the amount of trouble I was in this time it'd probably be my first name too. And my last. Trouble Mohammed Trouble Trouble. That's me.

Anyway, point is, I'd never seen my dad so angry, and I'd seen him angry a lot. He gets angry when he can't work the TV; he gets angry at wrong numbers; he gets angry when the toilet won't flush properly – hell, he gets angry over anything. But this was something else. He looked like his head might explode.

'Stand in the corner!' he shouted as he marched me through the front door of the house.

'Dad, please!' I said. 'You've got to listen to me!'

'Listen to you?' he shouted. 'Why would I listen to you? You never listen to me! You never do as I tell you! Perhaps thirty years in Pakistan with your uncle will give you a chance to think!'

'But, Dad!' I yelled.

Before I could finish, Mum stormed into the room.

For a second I thought she was there to defend me. Yeah, right.

'You!' she said, pointing a finger at me. 'I have just been on the phone with your Auntie Uzma. She tells me you have been mistreating your uncle!'

'What?' I replied. 'I haven't mistreated Grandpa!'

'Oh, really?' said my mother. 'I called Uzma to tell her how upset you had been about not seeing your uncle, and she told me what really happened.'

'"What really happened"?' I said. 'What's that meant to mean?'

'All you had to do was look after an old man, make him a cup of tea now and then, listen to his stories. Instead, you take him out all over town, fill his head with crazy ideas, leave him so exhausted that he is now bedridden! I don't know why I trusted you with so much responsibility!'

'But –' I tried to yell, but my dad was already yelling louder.

'Exactly! You have no discipline! You are unfit to be captain of my cricket team!'

'I never wanted to be captain!' I shouted. 'And I didn't do anything to Grandpa! He was the one who worked it out about the monsters in the first place!'

'*The monsters?*' said my mum, making a noise that would have been a laugh if she wasn't so angry. 'More of this? I thought you had grown out of these stories by now!'

'It ain't a story! It's true!' I shouted. 'It's the aunties! All of them! They're monsters! Creatures! Aliens! I don't know!'

'The aunties?' said my dad, and he did actually laugh this time. 'Are you a fool, boy? Do you think *I* am a fool? You try to make this about your auntie?'

'It *is* about her, and the rest of them. I swear – they're not human! Or they are but there's something controlling them. They've got a plan!'

'Humza! Stop!' shouted my mum. 'It's over! You have ruined the chance we gave you. You have let us down and let yourself down! There will be no money, no camera. It's finished. Now get to your room this instant. I am too angry to look at you!'

'But –' I began.

'GO!' they both shouted at once.

I sat down on my bed and put my head in my hands. It was a disaster. My mum was right – it was over. Everything was over. Grandpa was gone. The school was lost. The track was destroyed. We had no way of fighting back. No one would believe us. No camera, no future, no hope. Everything was lost.

And when I closed my eyes all I could see was those hundreds of faces, staring at me while I stood there on stage like a fool. I couldn't even do that right – the one thing I was most sure about. Even if the aunties weren't about to eat me or turn me into a slug or whatever they had planned, it didn't matter – I was never going to be a star. I just didn't have what it takes.

I don't know how many hours I sat there. No one came up with any lunch. No one came to talk it through. No one came at all. The sun eventually started to go down. I just lay there on my bed and waited until I could fall asleep. I didn't want to be awake any more.

I was just starting to doze off when I heard a loud beep. I jumped half out of my skin, before realizing that it was the pager. I pulled the little black box out of my bag and read the message:

YOU OK? CALL ME! UMER

Well . . . my parents hadn't said anything about not making phone calls. It wasn't like I could be in any worse trouble. Problem was, the only phone in the house was in the hallway downstairs. I'd have to be real quiet if I was gonna do this without getting caught.

I opened my door as silently as I could and stuck my head out. There was no one around. I could just about hear the sound of the TV downstairs. It was as good a time as any. I've learned that the quietest way to sneak down a staircase is with your feet at either edge, never in the middle. One step at a time, I made my way down to the hallway. Not a creak. I was doing well so far.

Once at the bottom of the stairs, I tiptoed to the phone and dialled Umer's number. He answered straight away.

'Humza?' said Umer, sounding worried.

'Yeah, it's me,' I replied in a near whisper.

'Are you OK?' he asked.

'Not really,' I said. 'We lost it. We lost the track.'

'I know,' he said, and you could hear the full weight of what that meant in his voice. 'I'm sorry.'

'Me too,' I replied. 'But it wasn't your fault. It was mine.'

'No it wasn't, Humza. It was just bad luck –' he

started to say, before I heard the creak behind me.

'What are you doing down here?' yelled my dad. He looked just as angry as he had that morning.

'I . . .' I started. 'I gotta go,' I said to Umer, and slammed the phone down. I turned to face my dad. That's when I saw the box beside him. It was about the size of a washing machine, made of wood and had air holes drilled in it in a few places.

'You've got to be kidding!' I said.

'This?' he replied, glancing at the crate. 'Absolutely not. I told you, if you continued to behave this way, I would ship you to Pakistan. You have forced my hand.'

'You can't ship me in a box! That's illegal,' I shouted.

'I have contacts at shipping authority. They will make exception for you.'

'I'll starve to death!'

'Ha!' he laughed. 'You are in no danger of starving, boy. Look at you!'

Damn, that was a low blow, even for him.

'Mum'll never let you do it,' I replied. 'Even if she *is* angry with me, she's not gonna let you send me to Pakistan in a wooden crate.'

'I make the decisions in this house!' he shouted,

before adding: 'Plus, your mother is out visiting Uzma, so what can she do? Now get in the crate!'

'I ain't getting in no crate,' I replied, stepping back.

'I won't seal it yet,' said my dad, stepping towards me. 'It is just to check measurements.'

'No way! You're crazy!' I yelled, taking another step back towards the door.

'Nonsense!' he yelled, advancing. 'I am the only sane one here!'

I felt the door handle against my back. I had nowhere to go. This insane old man was going to make me get in his box and there was nothing I could do. And then I heard it. A key turning in the lock behind me. The door began to push inward. I leapt to the side. It was Mum! I was saved!

'Oh, hello, dear,' said my dad in a cheerful voice, as he moved to stand in front of his crate.

'Hello, my darlings,' said my mum with a big smile on her face.

'Darlings'? Did she just say '*darlings*'? Like, two of us? Plural? Was I a 'darling' again? Was I out of trouble? What had happened?

Mum stepped inside. She had a big tray of Uzma's gulab jamun under one arm and she placed it down on the hall table as she entered.

'There we are,' she said, smiling. 'A nice treat for us all.'

'What, even the boy?' said my dad, sounding confused.

'Of course for the boy,' she said with a light, happy laugh. 'He needs feeding up!'

She turned towards me and took my cheeks in both hands.

'He is far too skinny,' she added.

My blood ran cold. My heart pounded in my chest. Looking into my mum's eyes – seeing the strange smile spread across her face – I knew beyond a shadow of a doubt: they'd got to her too.

My mum was one of them.

CHAPTER ELEVEN
TERRIBLE, TERRIBLE, TERRIBLE!

Breakfast was ridiculous. My mum must have been up half the night cooking. And it wasn't just breakfast foods – it was everything. Yeah, there were eggs and toast and cereal and pastries and all of that. But on top of that there were like six different curries, rice, pakora, samosas, laddoo, gulab jamun. I swear, the table legs were bowing under the weight of it all.

Mum watched me the whole time I was eating; that weird smile, those mad eyes. Eventually I told her I was full and was going to be late for school.

'Oh, they won't mind if you are a few minutes late,' she replied. 'Breakfast is the most important meal of the day. And so is lunch. And dinner. And snacks.'

I nodded and took one more small bite of

the sugary pastry I'd been eating.

'I gotta run,' I said.

'I will be preparing you an extra-special dinner tonight,' she said, smiling down at me, 'to make up for your difficult day yesterday. Won't that be nice, hmm?'

'Uh, yeah, great,' I said, grabbing my school bag. 'Can't wait.'

This was bad. I couldn't get out of there fast enough. It might have taken me a while to spot it with Auntie Uzma, but I could tell with my eyes shut that this *thing* wasn't my mum. No wonder Grandpa had figured it out so quick. I guess it's the people closest to you that are the easiest to spot.

Umer and Wendy were already waiting at the school gates when I arrived.

'Are you OK?' said Wendy.

'They got my mum,' I told her.

'What?' they both gasped at once.

'She went out last night and when she got home she was different. She's one of them.'

'Are you sure?' asked Umer.

'Positive. One minute she wanted to kill me, the next she was feeding me deep-fried sugar.

She's one of them.'

'Oh, man,' said Umer.

'This is bad,' added Wendy.

'Tell me about it,' I replied. 'Without the track, we're done for.'

'But there must be a way,' said Wendy. 'There must be a way we can convince someone we're telling the truth.'

'Who?' I replied. 'Who can we trust for sure? Even if we could guarantee that person wasn't a slug, how do we know they wouldn't go talk to my mum? She'd just say I was just making it up, and then they'd be on to us.'

The others went quiet as they thought about this.

'Our only shot was to expose them and it didn't work,' I said. 'I was wrong. Hell, I should have never even been up there. I ain't no rapper. I've ruined everything.'

'Of course you haven't, Humza,' said Umer, putting a hand on my shoulder. 'The track didn't do what we thought it was gonna do. Nothing happened. That's not your fault.'

'Umer's right,' said Wendy. 'The reaction can't have been caused by the bassline frequency, as I initially thought, because it had no effect on them. It must have been something else.'

She was right. Why *hadn't* it happened this time? Maybe it was never the track. Maybe it was something completely different that had caused the reaction in Mrs Masood.

'Humza,' said Wendy a moment later. 'When it happened before, in the library, you said it started as soon as you began playing the track, right?'

'Uh-huh.'

'Tell me again,' said Wendy.

'I was sat on the floor. I hit PLAY, the bass and the beat all started playing. I was just thinking that my lyrics were actually pretty good, when *bang!* – a book hit me on the head. That's when I looked up and saw Mrs Farooqi freaking out.'

'Your vocal –' said Wendy, 'does it come in right at the start of the song?'

'No,' I replied. 'There's, like, ten seconds of instrumental first.'

Wendy was quiet for a moment. Her mouth fell open.

'It's not just the bass . . .' she said. 'It's not just the music. It's *you*!'

'Me? What you talking about?'

'I thought it was the frequency of the music, of Mr Turnbull's unusual bassline, but it's the whole song! And *you're* part of the song! Your voice is part of that frequency!'

'You mean, it needed me to work?' I asked.

'Exactly! It wasn't until your voice came in that the frequency was just right. There must be something in the unusual high-pitched tone of your voice that mixes with that bassline to cause the reaction.'

'What you talking about, "unusual high-pitched tone"?' I replied.

'You do have kind of a weird voice,' agreed Umer. 'Especially when you rap.'

'What? No I don't!'

'It's sort of like a cartoon,' continued Umer. 'But, you know, in a good way. It's unique.'

A cartoon? What the hell was he talking about? What kind of rapper sounds like a cartoon? Man, I was an embarrassment. This was terrible.

Wendy had been quiet for a while, but then she lifted her eyes to stare at us. She looked like she might cry.

'That's the answer. The frequency of your voice. Because I removed the vocals yesterday the reaction never happened. That's why it didn't work. It's *my* fault!'

'No it ain't,' I replied. 'If I'd been able to perform it would have been fine. So it's still my fault.'

'But if I'd just left the track alone you wouldn't have had to perform at all. It's definitely *my* fault.'

'Trust me, Wendy, it's more my fault than it is yours.'

'It isn't!'

'It is!'

'IT ISN'T!'

'IT IS!'

'IT'S NO ONE'S FAULT!' shouted Umer, more forcefully than I'd ever heard him. 'We're fighting a bunch of monsters here! We don't know what we're doing. We're making it up as we go along and no one will help us. Of course things are going to go wrong!'

We both stared at him, too surprised to speak.

'Wendy, you couldn't have known what part of the track was going to work before now. It's why you're so good at science and figuring stuff out – because you always experiment until you *do* know. Until you understand. And, Humza,' he continued, turning to me, 'you're too hard on yourself.

That's why you couldn't perform yesterday. You put so much pressure on becoming famous and rich and everyone loving you – of course you're going to freeze up. You don't need to be famous to be liked. You're my best friend. I don't care if we make music or not. I don't care if you get famous. I don't care about any of it. I like you anyway.'

I didn't know what to say. I just stared at Umer's big warm face and knew that, somehow, he was right.

'Me too,' said Wendy a moment later. 'I never thought we'd be friends. But I'm glad we are.'

'Thanks, guys,' was all I managed to say.

It must have been windy out, because I suddenly realized my eyes were watering a little and I had to blink quite a lot to shift it. (Just to be clear, I ain't cried since I was six – so don't even go there.)

Standing at the school gates with my two best friends, I had no idea what we were going to do next. I didn't know how to fix any of this. All I knew was that it all suddenly felt a bit less scary.

School felt different again that day. There were just as many aunties, just as much food, but the mood had shifted – for us three at least. Yesterday we had a plan, we had a way of resisting them. Today we had nothing. Today the aunties were winning.

Kids didn't play in the playground any more. They just sat on the floor in little groups, sweating in the sunshine and eating sticky buns and toffee apples. And it was aunties as far as the eye could see. No dinner ladies, no teachers, no caretakers. Just colourful, cuddly aunties. Those mad eyes and weird grins.

Lessons were no better. The three of us just kept our heads down – ate as little as possible, said as little as possible. It was like we were just waiting for the end. Or maybe, just maybe, waiting for them to slip up. Waiting for another opportunity. But I couldn't see how that was going to happen. They were too crafty. We still had no idea what they were up to. If we couldn't get to the bottom of it, we were done for.

At the end of the day the three of us trudged out of school in silence. I don't know what either of the others were thinking – whether they were still trying to work out a solution, or if they were just feeling as stuck as I was. Whatever the case, it was Umer who saw it first.

'Uh, Humza,' he said.

I looked up to see what he was staring at. Standing next to his car at the front gate was my dad. His arms were folded, his expression grim – but somewhere in his eyes I could see that little twinkle he gets before dishing out a punishment. Man, this was just what I didn't need right now.

'Get in the car,' he barked.

'I can just walk home with these guys,' I replied. 'I don't need a lift.'

'I am not here to give you a lift. We are not going home,' he said, opening the passenger door.

I turned to the others. They could smell the danger in the air too.

'Good luck,' said Umer.

'Thanks,' I replied.

'See you tomorrow?' said Wendy.

I don't think she meant it to sound like a question but I guess she couldn't help it.

'Yeah, see you tomorrow,' I answered, then climbed into the car.

Minutes later we screeched to a halt outside a row of shops on the high street. Across the road, in the window of the electrical shop, I could see the video camera. Still on sale. Still twinkling in the light. I shook my head.

It all seemed like a long time ago now.

I felt pretty confident my dad hadn't driven me here on a surprise shopping trip though.

'Out,' he said.

I opened my door and stepped out of the car. I looked around the shopfronts, trying to figure out which of these places he was taking me to. The butcher's to chop me up? The baker's to incinerate me? The chemist's to poison me? Turns out it was none of these. It was the last place I'd have guessed.

'Get inside,' said Dad, holding open the door of the travel agent's.

'Why are we at a travel agent's?' I asked him. 'We ain't going on holiday.'

'No – *we* aren't,' he replied, pushing me through the door. '*You* are.'

I could see a familiar-looking woman sitting behind the counter. Mrs Hamid, I think. This was her and her husband's place. We always came here for our tickets to Pakistan . . .

Oh no.

'Dad, please don't do this,' I begged him.

He wasn't listening.

'Your mother says I cannot send you to Pakistan in a shipping container, even though it is excellent value. She is mad. But she cannot argue with aeroplane. Now sit down while I speak to Mrs Hamid.'

'Dad!' I cried, but it was no good.

'Silence!' he said, and he pushed me into one of the seats beside the door, before turning to the woman at the desk.

Fantastic. On top of everything, I was now about to be sent to live in Pakistan (probably the one place in the world where there were more Pakistani aunties than at my school). What was the point in even protesting? You never had any say as a kid. Life was just something that happened to you. You just tried to survive for as long as you could.

I sat there feeling numb to it all, staring at the pictures on the wall. No pictures of Pakistan, unsurprisingly. They were all the kinds of holiday destinations people might actually want to go to – big full-size wall prints of mountains, waterfalls and canyons.

Mountains . . .

Waterfalls . . .

Canyons . . .

I knew these pictures from somewhere. I got up and read the captions:

MOUNT FUJI
NIAGARA FALLS
THE GRAND CANYON

My jaw fell open so hard it nearly came off. The last thing Grandpa said. The teachers' holidays. It all made sense. How could I have missed it? This was the answer! This was the link!

I was out the door and running down the street before my dad could even get to his feet. I heard him shouting after me.

'You cannot stop this, boy! You are going to Pakistan! *Pakistaaaaan!*'

The words followed me round the corner and echoed in my head for at least three blocks. But it didn't matter now. I had something. I had proof!

If I was quick I could still catch Umer and Wendy on their walk home. The two of them went the same way as far as Tunnoch Street, before splitting off in the direction of their own homes. That's where I could intercept them. I ran like the wind (if the wind was a bit chubby from eating badly and not getting that much exercise).

I got there just in time to see them turning away from one another.

'Wait!' I shouted.

They stopped dead, turning to face me at the same time. I sprinted over, out of breath but desperate to explain.

'Pictures . . .' I gasped 'Fake! . . . Holidays . . . teachers . . . Not real!' I added.

They both looked at me, puzzled.

'Are you OK?' said Wendy.

'What did your dad do to you?' asked Umer.

'He took me . . .' I managed to say, 'to the travel agent's.'

'Travel agent's?' said Wendy. 'Why?'

'Doesn't matter . . . Pakistan . . . Not the point,' I said, shaking my head. 'Grandpa's last words . . . about the holidays . . . he figured it out . . .'

'Figured what out?' said Umer.

'They faked the holiday photos . . .' I explained, my breath beginning to come back. 'They used the photos at the travel agent's . . . Mrs Hamid must be in on it . . . They used the big photos on the wall there . . . Made it look like the teachers are on holiday . . . But it's all a lie . . . The online pictures are fake!'

'That's interesting,' said Wendy, 'but how does it help us?'

'Don't you see? It's proof. Proof there's a plot,' I replied.

Neither of them looked convinced.

'I know it doesn't seem big, not compared to giant slugs or whatever, but now we know how they're covering it up. We can use it against them!'

'How?' asked Umer.

'We can catch them in the act,' I replied. 'When they next take someone there to fake a photo we'll be there to watch them do it.'

'Stake out the travel agent's?' said Wendy.

'Exactly!' I replied.

'But how does that help us?' asked Umer.

'Because we can follow them,' I replied. 'Find out where they're taking everyone. Find their base. Find Grandpa!'

'But we don't know if they even have a base,' said Umer. 'What if they're just eating everyone?'

'Yeah, well hopefully they ain't just eating 'em. But if they are, we can find out where they're eating 'em. That's got to be proof enough to get the police involved.'

The others thought about it. Wendy was nodding.

'We can do it,' she said. 'We'll all need to be there in case we have to take breaks for the bathroom or whatever. And it could take a long time. We'll need an excuse. A reason to be out so long.'

'Can we say we're eating at yours?' I asked her. 'We can say we're watching a movie afterwards.'

'Uh . . . sure,' said Wendy, smiling.

'What?' I asked.

'Nothing,' she replied. 'I just don't usually have friends over for dinner.'

'This sounds kind of fun,' said Umer. He was smiling too.

'It could be dangerous,' I said. 'If they catch us, who knows what they'll do.'

They were both quiet for a time.

'But you still want to do it, right?' said Wendy.

'Course I do!' I said, grinning. 'One way or another, we're gonna take these aunties down!'

Wendy called her mum to ask if it was OK if her friends came over. Her mum was so happy to hear she had friends she didn't question it for a minute. I phoned my slug-mum to ask her if I could go to Wendy's for a 'cake and ice cream' party, followed by a movie (and more ice cream). She bought it hook, line and sinker.

'Oooh!' she squealed. 'That sounds like a marvellous idea! It is about time we got some meat on those bones!'

'Yeah, nice one, Mum,' I said, and hung up. 'Man, it is weird talking to that thing. It sounds exactly like her, but it just ain't.'

'It'll be OK,' said Umer, accepting his phone back. 'This isn't over yet.'

I nodded. It felt good to have a plan again.

Once Umer had let his mum know, we headed to Wendy's to get supplies for the stake-out.

Fact. Linda Wang is my new favourite person. No question.

All mums should be Wendy's mum. She was so nice to us! She wasn't strait-laced like I thought she would be. She wasn't like Wendy at all. She was fun.

'*Youuuu!*' she said, tearing the door open as we walked up the path. I thought for a second she was angry, but she wasn't. She was over the moon. 'I can't believe you've been keeping your good friends a secret from your mum!' she said, and grabbed me and Umer, dragging us into a big hug.

'Mum!' said Wendy. 'Less!'

'Oooh, I'm in trouble with Wendy Wang!' She laughed, with a fake guilty look on her face.

Ha! Even her mum called her by her full name. I liked Linda Wang immediately.

In the kitchen she put out a snack for us, and at first I was going to refuse out of habit, but when I saw what it was I couldn't help myself. Celery sticks and a low-fat yoghurt dip. Disgusting, right? I know. A few months ago I'd have run a mile. But now? Now it was amazing! It tasted clean. There was no sugar or fat. It wasn't deep-fried or dipped in chocolate. It was like a tall glass of water after a trek through the desert. Thank goodness for Linda Wang.

'So what are you kids going to do, huh?' asked Linda Wang. 'Would you like to see a movie or play video games? Or just watch a boring documentary with Wendy?'

'Mum,' said Wendy, looking annoyed.

'Oh, you know you love a boring documentary,' she said, and laughed.

Me and Umer, we laughed too. Then Wendy laughed.

'They're not boring. Not to me,' she said, smiling. 'But we're going out. We've got a project to work on.'

'Oh, so much schoolwork,' said Linda, shaking her head. 'You have friends here. Play a game. Run around. You will be old soon. Go and have fun.'

'I *am* having fun,' said Wendy, sounding irritated again. 'Sort of,' she added.

'What sort of project are you doing? Need Mum's help?' asked Linda Wang.

'No, we're just doing a survey on the high street,' replied Wendy, who seemed to be running out of patience with her mum.

'I'll drive you!' said Linda.

'It's five minutes' walk from here,' said Wendy. 'We'll be fine.'

'Hang on, Wendy,' I said. 'Maybe a car wouldn't be a bad idea. It'd be more like a proper stake-out. Give us some cover.'

'Yeah, but . . .' replied Wendy, 'she . . .'

'I'd like to sit in a car,' said Umer. 'I don't mind if your mum comes.'

'Aww, come on . . .!' said Wendy.

'Then it's agreed! Mum is part of the team!' said Linda Wang, and she high-fived Umer and me.

Wendy left her mum hanging, but Linda didn't seem to mind.

Ten minutes later we were parked up outside Hamid's travel agent's, watching passers-by come and go. Linda was already bored.

'I'm bored! I'm going to buy a magazine,' she said, opening her door. 'Don't talk to any strangers,' she added, 'unless they seem fun.'

Then she was gone.

'Why did you invite her along?' snapped Wendy. 'How are we meant to do this with my mum here?'

'She's OK,' I said, grinning. 'I like Linda Wang.'

'Plus, you've got a nice car,' added Umer, bouncing up and down on the seat.

'Urgh . . . Fine,' said Wendy, her arms folded, 'but let's not say too much in front of her. Trust me, we're better off if she's not overly involved.'

'So what happens now?' said Umer.

'Now we wait,' I replied. 'Watch for anything out of the ordinary. Clusters of aunties, that kind of thing. They've got to show up sooner or later.'

'Right,' said Wendy, 'but, if my mum asks, we're just doing a study on pedestrians. Measuring average height or something. She'll lose interest fast.'

'You're not really like her, are you?' I said.

'No,' she replied quickly. 'I'm not.'

And that's all she said on the subject.

An hour later we'd not seen any aunties. All of us were losing interest, but no one as much as Linda Wang. She'd read her magazine twice and completed the word search in the back.

'I'm *borrrrrred*, Wendy,' she moaned. 'Let's go bowling.'

'You can go bowling if you want. We need to stay here,' said Wendy through gritted teeth.

'Ahhhh . . .' groaned her mum, and she flipped back to the start of the magazine.

Outside the car, people made their way in and out of shops. I recognized the odd face. No one looked out of place – no weird smiles, no crazy eyes. Just normal people going about their afternoon. Linda Wang was right: this was pretty boring.

Then, out the corner of my eye, I spotted something. A flash of colour, a blur of movement. We all clocked it at once. Aunties. A pack of them. Six at least. They were waddling down the street in a little clump. Blue, yellow, pink, orange – all the colours of the classic Asian auntie, brilliant against the grey concrete of the high street.

But most importantly of all they were surrounding
something. Something big. There was someone
walking between them. And, despite the distance,
it was clear in an instant who it was.

'Mr Offalbox!' gasped all three of us at once.

'They finally got him,' I said.

They were wobbling up the street towards us,
taking funny little steps. They looked like a group
of pigeons when they try to run away from you
without flying. They bumbled and weaved in and

out among one another as they shepherded their enormous prize up the street. They were heading in the direction of the travel agent's. I had my fingers crossed that I was right about all this.

'Come on . . . come on . . .' I said.

Closer and closer they waddled. Closer and closer to the front door. Closer and closer to our car. We all sank a little in our seats as they drew up, but they didn't spot us. Instead they came to a stop right outside the travel agent's. And then, one at a time, they began to file inside.

Mr Offalbox didn't look himself as he shuffled past us. His eyes were dopey and half closed. It was the same look the teachers had worn in their holiday photos. He was letting himself be led along without any protest. This was definitely it! They were here for the cover-up!

'You were right!' said Wendy. 'You were right!'

'What's going on?' asked Linda.

'Shh!' snapped Wendy.

Linda shook her head and went back to her magazine. We sat in silence and watched. It was hard to see what was going on inside. It was just a mess of colour and movement as the aunties shuffled around the place. Then came a bright camera flash, followed by two more. And, a moment after that, the door opened and the aunties began to spill back out.

'They've done it,' said Wendy. 'They've taken the photos.'

'Linda Wang,' I said. 'Follow those aunties.'

'Huh?' replied Linda, looking up.

'You heard him, Mum,' snapped Wendy. 'We need to tail that group of middle-aged Pakistani women.'

There was a short pause as Linda Wang considered this request.

'OK,' she said with a smile, and started the engine.

We crawled down the road behind them, keeping a safe distance. The odd car beeped at Linda for driving so slowly, but she just shouted at them out the window.

'Go round! Go round!' she yelled. 'We're doing homework!'

The aunties never looked back though. Wherever they were heading, they were going there as fast as their stubby little legs could carry them. And the headmaster was still right there at their centre.

We followed them off the high street and along

a number of smaller roads. They were the kind of local streets you were sure you'd been down at some point, but couldn't really remember when. There were fewer shops and houses here. The handful of businesses that remained open looked rough and kind of filthy. One was burned out, another was just an empty lot filled with rubble. It wasn't the sort of neighbourhood you'd normally expect to find a nice group of aunties in. But that didn't seem to stop them. They just waddled on like the penguins in that documentary about penguins.

And then they were gone – in through the front door of a big, dirty old warehouse. Linda Wang rolled to a slow stop.

'That was fun,' she said, looking round at us. 'Who shall we follow next?'

'No one,' said Wendy. 'Now we stay here and observe.'

'Oh, come on!' said her mum. 'We've been doing that for hours. Let's go and see a movie.'

'This is important, Mum!' said Wendy. 'We need to see what they do next . . . for our, uh, homework.'

'This is weird homework,' said Linda Wang, shifting her position until she was lower in her seat. 'I'm going to sleep. You're boring, Wendy Wang.'

And, with that, she shut her eyes and started to doze off.

'What do you think it is?' asked Umer in a whisper.

'Don't know,' I replied. 'Some sort of head-quarters maybe?'

'Do you suppose this is where they've taken all the teachers?' whispered Wendy.

'It must be,' I said.

'But what for?' said Umer.

We sat there staring at the big dirty building and imagined what could possibly be going on in there. We knew there was only one way to find out.

We had to get inside.

CHAPTER TWELVE
THE WAREHOUSE

An hour later the aunties reappeared. It was dark now and their colourful dresses looked dull in the grey-orange street light. Mr Offalbox was nowhere to be seen.

'They've left him behind,' whispered Wendy, careful not to wake her mum.

Linda Wang was snoring away beside her and hadn't stirred in ages. This was our chance.

The little group of aunties began to shuffle down the street, popping in and out of view as they slipped beneath the street lights. When they were far enough away, we opened the doors and stepped out into the night. Wendy tore a page from her schoolbook and scribbled a message on it for her mum. It read:

If we're not back by 9 call the police!

We had no idea what was about to happen but we all knew we couldn't go back. Every day there was less and less to go back to. Somehow I knew in my bones that this place was the heart of it. This was where the answers lay.

'How are we going to get inside?' asked Umer.

'We could try the front door?' I suggested.

It was no good though. The aunties had locked it up tight. Even with my face pressed to the glass, I couldn't see a thing inside. We had to find another way in. We set off to hunt around the edges of the building.

'Maybe we should just call the police?' said Umer.

'And tell 'em what?' I asked him. 'We saw some aunties in a bad neighbourhood and got suspicious, so would you mind kicking in a door for us?'

'We're getting in a bit over our heads is all,' he said.

'We ain't got a choice. Not any more. If this is where they've taken everybody, then this is where we need to be.'

'Agreed,' said Wendy. 'The answers are in here.

We have to get inside.'

And that's when we spotted it – all three of us at once. A half-open window, five or six feet off the ground.

'Someone, give me a boost,' I said.

They both just stared at me.

'What?'

'No way we can lift you,' said Wendy.

'I ain't that heavy! I've been watching my weight! Now come here and pick me up!'

'There's a dustbin over there,' said Umer. 'Can't you just stand on that?'

'Fine,' I muttered, walking over to the bin. 'But I'm light as a feather.'

Flipping the metal can over and standing on its end gave me just enough height to reach the window. I pushed it open and peered inside. It was pretty dark – I couldn't really tell what I was looking at. I glanced about the street one last time to make sure we were still alone.

'Right, I'll see you in there,' I said, and began hoisting myself over the window frame.

'Be careful,' said Umer.

'Course, man, I always – *aarrrghghh!*' I yelled, as I fell head first into the warehouse. I bounced off something hard and spun through the darkness, landing in a heap on the floor.

'Humza?' shouted Umer. 'Are you OK?'

'Urgnn . . .' I groaned.

I couldn't make out what had broken my fall. Some sort of table or counter maybe? Climbing on to it and standing on tiptoes, I pulled myself back up to the window ledge. I popped my head out and looked down at the others.

'Are you hurt?' asked Wendy.

'Don't worry about it,' I replied. 'There's a table or something in here. We'll use it to get back out.'

I reached a hand down to help pull Umer up to the window ledge. Wendy pushed his bum and I tugged his arms with all my might. I couldn't see why they'd brought up *my* weight. Have you ever seen a hippo birth? That's pretty much how it looked when Umer finally plopped through the window and into my arms. We fell over backwards with a crash and lay there panting like dogs in a hot car.

Of course, when it came to Wendy's turn, like everything else in life, she made it look easy, slipping through the gap and landing on her feet before we'd even had a chance to pick ourselves up from Umer's belly-flop.

When all three of us were inside, Wendy whipped out a powerful little torch and flipped it on. The room lit up. This was not what I was expecting. Firstly, the table wasn't a table. It looked like a computer of some sort. And not like any I'd ever seen before. Weird displays and flashing lights peppered a control panel so complex it gave me a headache just to look at it. The rest of the room was lined in dark, smooth metallic panels. It did *not* resemble the inside of a rundown warehouse. Not one bit.

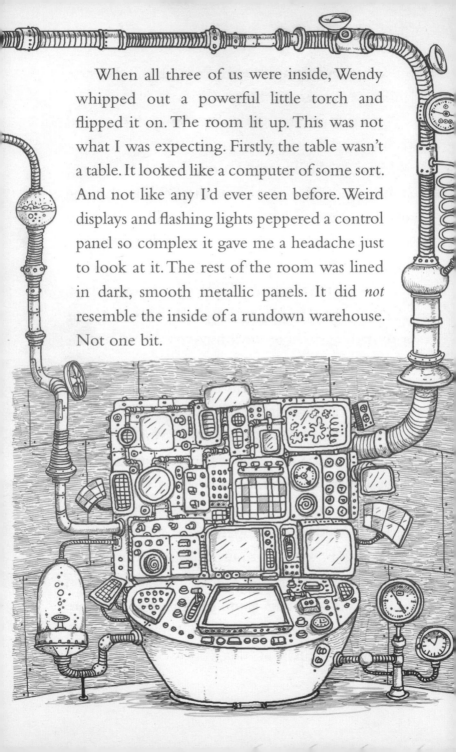

'What is this place?' said Umer.

'I have no idea,' I replied, taking it all in.

'It looks futuristic,' said Wendy. '. . . Advanced technology.'

'Aliens . . .' whispered Umer.

No one said a word. Was that it? Was that the answer? Were these horrible slug-like creatures from outer space? They certainly didn't look like anything from Earth. Somehow, all of a sudden, I was sure of it. We were dealing with extraterrestrials.

'This is bad,' said Wendy. 'This is really bad.'

'It ain't good,' I agreed. 'Let's get out of here as quick as we can. We just need to find Grandpa first.'

'Right,' said Wendy, and she pointed her torch towards the distant hallway. 'After you,' she added.

'Umer,' I said, 'you can go first if you like.'

'Me?' replied Umer. 'No way – he's *your* Grandpa.'

'No he ain't! He's my uncle.'

'Good enough for me,' said Wendy.

'Lead the way,' said Umer.

Man, these two chickens were gonna make me take all the risks. Fine, whatever. I wasn't scared . . .

I tiptoed out of the room and into the corridor. The walls and the floor were made of the same dark metal panels as the control station we'd seen. It looked like some weird, evil Apple Store. You wouldn't guess in a million years that all this was inside a crummy derelict warehouse in a bad part of town. It was a pretty smart hiding place. *Misdirection*, I thought to myself. Man, I hoped Grandpa was here.

Wendy's torch gave us just enough light to see where we were going, though we obviously had no idea where that was meant to be. All I could tell was that we were getting deeper into the building. Even being as quiet as we could, every footstep echoed about the place.

'I don't like this,' said Umer, under his breath.

'Of course you don't like it,' I replied. 'Why would anyone like this? I hate this. I'd rather be at school than here. I'd rather be playing cricket!'

'Let's just find him and get out,' said Wendy.

'Uh-huh,' agreed Umer. 'Those aunties could come back anytime.'

'Yeah . . . or maybe they're already here . . .' I added, and kinda wished I hadn't.

No one said a word after that, but we all moved a little faster.

It wasn't long before the corridor came to an end and we found ourselves up against a large metal door. There were no handles, no buttons – just a huge sealed hatch, blocking us from going any further.

'What now?' said Umer.

'We'll have to go back,' replied Wendy. 'Try the other way.'

'There must be some way to get through,' I told her. 'We just need to figure it out.'

'Figure it out?' said Wendy. 'It's super-advanced alien technology. They could have security systems we can't even conceive of. We'll never get through!'

As she said the last word, Wendy slapped the flat of her hand against the great metal door. The instant her skin touched its surface the door slid open with a hiss, moving so fast you could barely see it go. It took Wendy by such surprise that she lost her balance and stumbled forward into the room beyond. As she did, every light in the place flickered into life. A cold, blue glow filled the enormous space.

'Oh my . . .' said Wendy.

'I guess this is it . . .' said Umer.

And he was right. This had to be it. The space was huge. Cavernous. An aeroplane hangar filled with beds as far as the eye could see. Row after

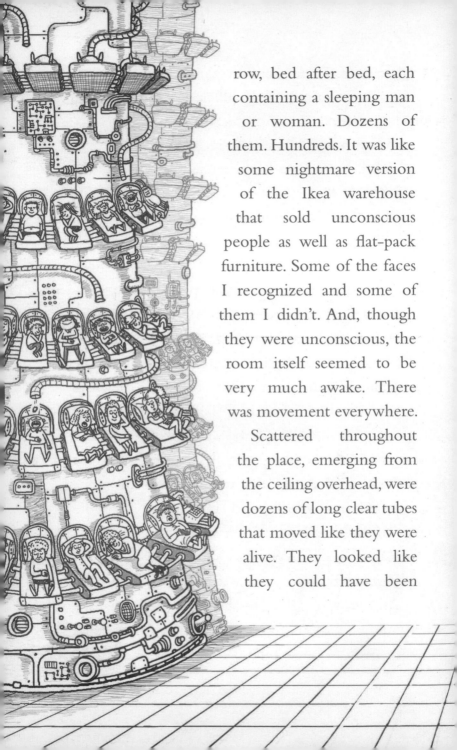

row, bed after bed, each containing a sleeping man or woman. Dozens of them. Hundreds. It was like some nightmare version of the Ikea warehouse that sold unconscious people as well as flat-pack furniture. Some of the faces I recognized and some of them I didn't. And, though they were unconscious, the room itself seemed to be very much awake. There was movement everywhere.

Scattered throughout the place, emerging from the ceiling overhead, were dozens of long clear tubes that moved like they were alive. They looked like they could have been made of glass, but somehow they were fluid, flexible. They twisted like tentacles as they swept about the place, whipping from one figure to the next. Each would stop briefly above a bed's sleeping inhabitant, peering in close for a moment, before racing off to another. They seemed to be observing the sleepers.

As we watched, one of the tubes nearby began to hum. The man in the bed beneath – a chubby little guy with a bushy beard – was stirring slightly. The tube had raced to him, spluttered for a moment, positioncd itself directly over his

mouth and dropped a jam doughnut into it. The guy chewed it for a moment, swallowed and fell back to sleep.

'They're feeding them . . .' said Umer.

'Fattening them up,' added Wendy.

'Yeah, and probably keeping 'em asleep too,' I said.

It was happening all over the room. These weird glass tentacle tubes from the ceiling were dropping little snacks into the mouths of anyone who so much as snored.

'We've got to find Grandpa,' I said. 'And quick.'

The others nodded. Without another word, we ran into the enormous room, each heading down a different row. There were so many of them. So many beds and so many faces. The few I did recognize had changed, and it took me a moment to realize how. They were all chubbier. Everyone in the room was ballooning. Their plan, whatever it was, was clearly working. The whole town was getting fat.

I saw an old man in a bed nearby and raced to his side. But it wasn't Grandpa. I realized I recognized him though: Mr Singh from the greengrocer's. It was definitely him, but he was almost too big for his turban now. I spotted another old guy a few beds away, but on closer inspection he turned out to be a woman (must have been a tough life, fam). I kept looking.

Bed after bed, row after row. No Grandpa. I began to worry that maybe he wasn't here. Maybe they'd got rid of him already – or had they taken him somewhere else? Maybe I was too late.

I looked up to see how Umer and Wendy were getting on, and that's when I saw him. He was maybe twenty beds away, fast asleep and snoring. I'd have barely recognized him. He must have put on three stone. His wrinkles had stretched tight, his sunken cheeks had filled in and his belly stood out so far he looked like he might have been expecting a whole litter of Grandpas. What had they done to him?

'Grandpa!' I said, grabbing him by the shoulder. 'Wake up, man!'

The others must have heard me because they ran over to join us.

'Grandpa!' I said again, and tried carefully to peel open one of his eyes.

I was worrying he might be out cold and that we'd have to try to carry him out of here when he suddenly gasped for air. His eyes bolted open and he looked right at me. For a second everyone froze. Then his mouth spread wide into a familiar snaggle-toothed grin. This wasn't the grin of any alien slug person. It was Grandpa. We'd found him in time.

'The holidays?' he croaked. 'You worked it out?'

'We did!' I shouted as I hugged him. 'We found the travel agent's. I saw the photos.'

'I knew you would . . .' he said, closing his eyes.

'Uh-uh!' I said, shaking him. 'Wake up, Grandpa. We're gonna get you out of here!'

Grandpa opened his eyes again, raising his head a little. The smile returned to his face. But, in that same moment, one of the glass tubes appeared out of the darkness overhead, racing down towards us. We all froze. The tube stopped, just inches from Grandpa's head, and began its gentle hum. It was feeding time. I looked up just in time to see a doughnut plummet down the shaft towards Grandpa.

'Get away from him!' I said, and slapped the tube with the back of my hand. The falling doughnut missed Grandpa and bounced on to the floor. The glass tube reacted almost like a person might, pulling back in surprise. For a moment it seemed almost to be watching me, working me out.

Then, as swiftly as it had appeared, it whipped away into the darkness. For a second or two nothing happened.

'That was close . . .' I said, a little too soon.

The blue lighting of the room faded to deep red. A dull, distant alarm began to sound. Uh-oh.

'We need to move now, Grandpa!' I shouted.

'I can't,' he replied. 'Look . . .'

I looked down to see that his arms were bound to the bed frame with some pretty serious-looking metal manacles.

'Ah, man,' I said, trying to prise them open with my fingers. They wouldn't budge.

'Humza,' came Wendy's voice, her hand on my shoulder. 'We have to go.'

'I'm not leaving him!' I shouted. 'Grandpa, can you squeeze out of 'em?' I asked.

He began to tug his wrists back through the holes of the manacles, and for a moment I thought he was gonna make it. It was so close. But his old thin skin was catching and if he pulled any harder his hands would be torn to shreds. He was stuck.

'Here,' said Umer, handing me something from the floor.

'What?' I snapped. 'Why you giving me this,

man? I don't need a doughnut! This ain't the time for food!'

'The jam,' he replied. 'Use the jam.'

It took me a moment to realize what the hell he was talking about. Then it clicked. The jam was runny! After that, I would never call Umer an idiot again. Yeah, his brain worked differently to mine, maybe even differently to most people's, but he could see things when other people missed them. And right now he was a genius.

I grabbed the doughnut from him and squeezed it hard, spraying half the jam over one of Grandpa's wrists and half over the other.

'Try again, Grandpa. Pull!' I shouted.

Grandpa pulled. Both arms at once, with all his strength. There was a moment's resistance, then a *pop!* and Grandpa's hands came free.

'Yes!' I cried.

'Help me up!' he said, and Umer and I each took an arm.

He was dressed in something like a hospital gown, presumably so they could fatten him up without his trousers bursting. He was a little wobbly on his feet to begin with but was soon keeping up by himself.

'What about everyone else?' said Grandpa, looking at the rows of other beds.

'There isn't time,' I replied. 'We'll have to come back for them.'

I was about to explain to him that this place was all the proof we needed – that now someone would have to listen – when the big metallic door at the far end of the room hissed open. Without a word, we ducked down among the beds. I peered out over the sleeping body in front of me.

Aunties . . . A dozen of them at least. They began to fan out into the room, hunting for the cause of the disturbance. None of us moved a muscle. If they looked straight at us we were done for. I held my breath. We all did. We had to let them get past us, then we could make a run for it. My heart was racing.

And then I saw them – eyes staring straight at me, just inches from my face. I came *that* close to screaming. But it was no auntie. I knew those eyes. Mr Turnbull! He was alive!

Somehow, among all these beds, I'd managed to duck down behind his. He must have been able to see the fear in my face, because he didn't make a sound. I put my fingers to my lips and made the 'shh!' sign. He gave a small sharp nod.

The closest auntie was now just ten feet away. She was looking at each of the sleepers, checking things were as they should be. Now she was within six feet of us. Five. Closer. I could feel sweat running down my brow. No one so much as breathed.

And then she was gone, hurrying away to another bed nearby.

'Get help,' whispered Mr Turnbull when she was out of earshot.

'We've gotta get you out of here,' I told him.

He shook his head.

'But, sir! We need you! It's the track. Our track. It's how we can beat them.'

He looked puzzled.

'It's something to do with the frequency of the music – the bass or something. I don't know. Wendy figured it out. It affects them somehow. Exposes them.'

He was listening, but didn't speak.

'I lost it, sir,' I continued. 'I lost the laptop. I lost the track. We can't get it back without you. You have to come.'

'Humza,' he whispered. 'If they catch you none of that'll matter. You need to run.'

I looked up to check on the aunties. They'd all moved past us now. They were nearly at Grandpa's bed. When they got there, they'd know he was loose. We had to move.

'I'll come back for you, sir, I promise.'

'I know you will,' he replied. 'Now go!'

I was about to turn when he spoke again.

'There's a backup,' he said. 'If you need it, there's a copy of the track.'

'A copy? Where?'

'Look in my drawer,' he replied. 'At the school. A memory stick. You'll see it.'

And then came the shout. One of the aunties had reached Grandpa's bed. It was now or never.

'Go!' he yelled.

And we ran. I didn't look back. Not once. I couldn't.

We were through the metal doors and tearing down the corridor in seconds. I kept an arm round Grandpa to make sure he didn't stumble in the darkness. He must have been in bed for days now, so was still pretty wobbly on his feet.

Umer and Wendy were already inside the little control room when we burst in through the door. They went first, out the window and into the street, ready to help Grandpa on the other side. I steadied him as he climbed on to the console and wriggled his way out the window. I could hear footsteps in the hallway behind me now. As soon as he was safely in Umer and Wendy's arms, I pulled myself up and over the window frame.

I felt something grab at my foot as I tumbled out through the window and into the street with a crash, knocking the dustbin over and spilling rubbish everywhere. There was too much adrenalin going through me to feel the fall. I was just glad I hadn't landed on Grandpa.

We ran back to where we'd left Linda Wang asleep in the car. She hadn't moved an inch and was snoring away in the driver's seat. We threw ourselves into the back seat as Wendy jumped in beside her mum.

'Drive!' she shouted, slamming her door.

'*Aarggghhhh!*' shouted Linda Wang, looking like she'd been electrocuted. She didn't pause to ask questions – just wrenched the key in the ignition and slammed down the accelerator. We shot off so fast even my dad would have struggled to keep up.

When we skidded to a halt two minutes later Linda finally stopped screaming.

'What the heck, Wendy?' she cried. 'What happened? Why are you screaming at me?'

'Mum,' replied Wendy firmly. 'I'd like you to meet Mr Khan. You can call him Grandpa.'

Linda turned slowly towards the back seat where Grandpa sat between us in his hospital gown, his hair and beard sticking up all over the place.

'Hello, missus,' he said with a little yellow grin.

She stared at him for a moment, as though trying to work out if maybe she was still dreaming.

'OK . . .' she eventually mumbled. 'I think I'll head home now . . .'

'Sorry, Linda Wang,' I replied. 'No can do. We gotta get to the police station, fast.'

She looked at me like she didn't even really understand the words. I guess she was probably still in shock – you know, with the whole 'waking up screaming' bit. Poor old Linda Wang. All she wanted to do was go bowling.

'Police station?' she mumbled.

'Police station!' all four of us barked at once.

She could see there was no winning this one. She nodded silently, flicking on the indicator, and she pulled away from the kerb.

I slid down in my seat. My heart was still

pounding in my chest. We were finally on the right path. Now that we had Grandpa the police would *have* to listen to us. How could they not?

Just in case you and your mates ever have to go into a police station before your twelfth birthday, escorting an old man who looks like he recently escaped from a mental health unit, intending to convince them that a bunch of aunties from the area are *actually* alien invaders who have kidnapped hundreds of local residents and are force-feeding them doughnuts in a warehouse downtown – let me give you some advice: don't bother.

'Well, well, well . . . Humza Khan,' said the officer at the front desk. 'You know we've got a file on you?'

'Eh?' I replied, a bit surprised (and maybe a bit excited) to hear this.

'Vampire lollipop lady, escaped python at Greggs, human eyeballs in the pic'n'mix . . . Any of these stories ring a bell?' he said, raising an eyebrow so high it nearly joined his haircut.

'Ah, come on! Those were genuine concerns!'

'You're a time-waster, Khan, just like your old man.'

'What's my dad got to do with this?'

'He's as bad as you are. He tried to convince me it was an escaped octopus that had been dumping all the Aldi trolleys in Peabody Pond. How do you even come up with this stuff?'

'Hey, come on – don't lump me with that guy; he's got issues. I'm just trying to do the right thing!'

'By reporting an alien invasion?'

'I swear! It's true! Tell him, Grandpa!'

'It's true,' said Grandpa. 'The aunties are aliens. They make me eat doughnuts.'

It wasn't the best defence I'd ever heard, but surely this guy had to believe Grandpa?

Nope. Turns out old people and kids get the same rubbish treatment.

'Are you meant to be in hospital, by any chance, sir?' the policeman asked Grandpa. 'Do you perhaps have a wife or a care worker we might call?'

'No!' I cried. 'His wife's one of them! So's my mum! Why aren't you listening?'

'We swear it's true!' said Umer.

'We wouldn't lie about something like this,' added Wendy.

The policeman stared at us all. He had a look

on his face that was somewhere between bored, annoyed and confused.

'Right,' he eventually said. 'Firstly, let me be very clear: I don't believe you. Not even slightly. But I'd not be doing my job if I didn't send a car out to this warehouse of yours to follow up.'

'Yes!' I shouted, and the others began to celebrate with me.

'Quiet!' he snapped. 'I'll send someone out with you to have a look. But, if I find you've wasted my time, there *WILL* be consequences. Understand?'

'I swear, you ain't gonna regret it,' I told him. 'They'll give you a medal for this!'

'Uh-huh,' said the desk sergeant, and he reached over to pick up his radio.

We carried on celebrating as he called it in. Finally this would all be over. That guy was gonna feel pretty stupid when he heard what we'd found . . .

It was impossible. Just . . . impossible . . .

'I don't understand . . .' said Wendy.

'Are we definitely in the right place?' asked Umer, looking about.

I couldn't even speak.

The whole thing, the entire warehouse, it was . . .

gone. Vanished. Just an empty lot; scattered rubble and cracked concrete. No building, no aunties, no beds. Nothing.

The police officers who had been sent along with us were standing next to their car, radioing back to the station. Grandpa was wandering back and forth near the spot where we'd climbed through the window. He was muttering to himself, examining the ground, inspecting fragments of debris. The bin we'd used to stand on was still right there, lying on its side.

'Can we go home?' said Linda Wang out of the car window.

'Just a minute, Mum,' said Wendy, before turning back to us. 'What do we do now? How can we convince them we're not lying?'

'I . . . I don't know . . .' I mumbled. 'I don't understand . . . How can a whole building just disappear into thin air?'

'Not building,' said Grandpa, walking over. 'Spaceship.'

'What?' All three of us gasped at once.

'We were never inside a building,' he said quietly. 'It was a spaceship all along.'

Grandpa didn't get long to explain everything

he'd seen. The police were insisting on driving me and Umer home – probably so we'd get in maximum trouble with our parents. But in the few minutes we had with Grandpa, he told us what he could.

'These aliens –' he said, 'when they are not aunties, they are slugs.'

'I know!' I yelled. 'I saw one!'

I was so relieved to hear that, finally, someone else had seen one too. 'It came out of the librarian,' I continued. 'I tried to warn people, but no one would listen.'

'Of course not,' Grandpa said. 'It is hard to believe. But these aliens are fattening us up. They need to feed us, feed us, feed us until there is plenty of room inside.'

'Room for what?' asked Umer.

'For them,' I replied.

'Mmm,' said Grandpa with a nod. 'You need great big round stomach for an alien to live in. Skinny people are no good.'

'That's why they picked aunties!' I gasped, suddenly getting it. 'No one would suspect a thing if they went around pushing food on people. It's classic auntie behaviour.'

'Exactly!' said Grandpa. 'Perfect disguise. And,

once you are big and fat and round enough, aliens climb in and take over. Drive you, like a car.'

'But why the school?' said Wendy. 'Why are they working so hard to fatten up a bunch of kids?'

'Next phase of invasion,' whispered Grandpa. 'Slug babies . . .'

We all stood in silence, taking it in. I mean, what can you say to something like that? One by one, they were converting us into walking slug nurseries.

'Right,' came an irritable voice from nearby. 'Get in the car. We're taking you lot home.'

The police officers were looking pretty annoyed at this point.

'Can we just have five more minutes?' I begged.

'What? No!' snapped the policeman. 'Of course you bloody can't. Now get in the car.'

But then he stopped and looked around. A puzzled expression fell across his face.

'Where's the old fella?' he asked.

We all turned to look. Apparently, it wasn't just coins he was good with.

Grandpa had vanished.

CHAPTER THIRTEEN
THE NEW CANTEEN

Things my dad is angry about:

No. 1:
Me getting an official caution from the police. Especially as they had a massive go at him for setting a bad example. Yeah, we all know he makes stuff up a lot, but we also know not to challenge him on it. He did not like the cops calling him a liar one bit. He was raging when they left.

No. 2:
Me running away from the travel agent's that afternoon. Dad was furious about this one. He shouted at me for twenty minutes about that alone. He even showed me the tickets he'd booked for next month to Pakistan. One way. In my name . . .

As soon as school was done, I was gone.

No. 3:
Me costing him that cricket game. Yup, that came back up again during the shouting. It had really hurt his pride. I was a bit surprised how much of his self-respect was based on that coach Siddiki guy and a cricket game from thirty years ago. Why was he putting that on me?

No. 4:
Mum not being as angry with me as he was. He couldn't get his head round why she was feeding me snacks and being nice to me while he had to keep his hands jammed in his pockets just to keep from tearing my ears off. There was no point explaining to him that this thing wasn't actually my mum and that the creature he'd been watching telly next to every night was really a big green alien slug. It would have just made him angrier.

No. 5 (and this is the big one):
We wouldn't know it until we arrived at school the next morning, but the aunties were about to make Dad angrier than ever before. They were going to

take away from him the one little thing that had been keeping him sane. The aunties had reached a decision . . .

'WHAT?!??!' came an earth-shaking cry from somewhere in the depths of the school.

The windows rattled and a board-marker rolled off Auntie Uzma's desk and on to the floor.

'Uh . . . is it just me . . .' said Umer, leaning over, '. . . or does that sound a lot like your dad?'

'It sounds *exactly* like my dad,' I replied, trying to figure out what else could possibly have gone wrong.

Moments later we heard a further commotion coming from the playground. The whole class looked out the window to see my dad being escorted off the premises by a gang of aunties.

'Do not touch me!' he shouted. 'This is unacceptable! You cannot do this!'

'I wonder what they did to make him so angry?' said Wendy.

'He's always angry,' I replied. 'He does this if you put the heating on before November.'

But somehow I knew this was bigger. This was something that had genuinely upset him. He looked like he might cry or bite someone.

'Cricket . . .' I said. 'It's got to be the cricket. They must have fired him or something.'

'Wow . . .' said Wendy, as she watched my father attacking the school gates with a tree branch. 'Your dad must really like cricket.'

'Miss,' I said, turning to the front of the room. 'I mean, Auntie?'

'What is it, Humza?' said Auntie Uzma, looking up from the cake she was decorating.

'Has anything happened with the cricket team?' I asked.

'Oh yes,' she replied, smiling. 'It's very good news. All the school sports have been suspended to make way for the new canteen.'

'New canteen?' said Wendy.

'That's right,' replied Auntie Uzma. 'A brand-new,

multi-storey, state-of-the-art school canteen! It will be so big and so efficient we will be able to ship in children from every school in the area and feed them to bursting!'

'What does that have to do with cricket?' I asked.

'Well,' said Auntie Uzma, 'it has to go somewhere, doesn't it? So where better than the horrible old playing field! All that exercise was making you all look so skinny and ill.'

'The playing field?' said Wendy. 'You're getting rid of the entire playing field? You can't do that!'

'It's already done,' said Auntie Uzma, smiling broadly. 'See?'

She pointed out of the far window, past the tarmac area of the playground, towards where the playing field had always been. But there was no playing field any more. No grass, no goals, no kids doing sport. Just a huge, brand-new, state-of-the-art canteen.

'It's impossible . . .' said Wendy, removing her glasses, as though they might be the problem.

There had been no construction work, no builders, no lorries – nothing at all. Yesterday it was the playing field, today it was a shiny glass building, as tall as the school. It was like it had appeared out of nowhere.

'The ship!' All three of us gasped at once – though not quite loud enough to be heard by Auntie Uzma.

It had to be. There was no other explanation. They'd parked their ship right here in the school and disguised it again to fit in with its surroundings.

'But you are not to go in there until the night of the grand opening,' said Auntie Uzma in a stern tone. 'There is still work going on inside and it is dangerous for children.'

'*I bet it is,*' whispered Wendy.

'When is that, miss? The grand opening,' I asked.

'Why, the night of the talent show – tomorrow!'

she answered with a grin. 'No more dingy old assembly hall for us! We shall be holding the entire event in our beautiful new canteen.'

'We're having the talent show *inside* that thing?' I said, trying not to sound concerned.

'Won't it be wonderful!' said Auntie Uzma, glowing.

Umer, Wendy and I exchanged a worried look.

'And don't forget: attendance is compulsory,' she added. 'Now, who would like a slice of cake?'

'Did you hear her?' said Wendy, the moment we were alone at break. 'Attendance is compulsory! They're planning to turn us all at once!'

'I don't want to be a slug person!' cried Umer.

'What are we going to do?' said Wendy. 'How are we going to stop them?'

They were both looking at me like I had the answer.

Luckily, I did.

'With the track,' I replied in a voice that sounded calmer than I felt. 'There's still one copy left and we're gonna get it. If attendance is compulsory for us, you can bet every last one of them's gonna be there too. So that's when we hit back.'

'You mean . . .' said Umer.

'Uh-huh,' I said with a nod, '. . . we're entering the talent show.'

And that was it. We had a plan. And it wasn't just any plan — it was a last-ditch, no-room-for-error, fail-and-we-die kind of plan. If it went wrong this time, they won. More schools would get taken over. More aunties, more teachers, more kids — all becoming slug people. First Eggington, then England, then the world. We had to stop them. We couldn't fail.

But there wasn't much time to get organized. We'd have to get on it, fast! We found the sign-up sheet for the talent show pinned to the notice board, exactly where Mr T had left it. There was a single blank box left at the bottom; room for one more entry. I took up the pen that was dangling beside it and signed my name.

'Here you go, Umer,' I said, holding it out towards him.

'Me?' he replied. 'Are you sure? I only have to hit PLAY. You're the one up on stage.'

'I can't do it without you, man,' I told him.

Umer smiled and took the pen. He carefully added his name beside mine.

'You too, Wendy,' I said, nodding at the pen in Umer's hand.

'What?' she replied. 'It's not my song.'

'If this works,' I said, 'it's only because we did it together.'

Umer held out the pen towards her, a goofy grin on his face. Wendy looked at the pen for a moment. Then, smiling back at us, took it and signed her name.

'Right,' I said, turning towards the music room. 'Now for the track . . .'

Inside Mrs Jahib's classroom, three dozen chubby-looking Year Twos were digging into the centre of a massive sticky toffee pudding.

They'd help themselves to a spoonful, then, while they chewed, pick up a triangle and ding it once, before returning to the pudding. This wasn't a music lesson – it was a joke! The aunties weren't even pretending to teach us any more. And check out all the tummies in there! I doubted there was a single stomach left in the school that wouldn't make a nice studio flat for an alien slug. This had to end, now!

'Do you need me to dress up as a ghost again?' asked Umer.

'Not this time,' I told him. 'The way I see it, MrT said the memory stick's ours. So we're taking it.'

I turned the handle and marched into Mrs Jahib's class. She looked up, startled.

'You again!' she said. 'What are you doing here?'

I walked straight to MrT's desk and pulled open the drawer. There it was: the little white plastic memory stick he used for backups. I grabbed it before Mrs Jahib could even see what it was.

'What have you got there?' she demanded.

'Fudge,' I said, spinning round to face her. 'Mr Turnbull's delicious homemade fudge. He always hides it there.'

There was a moment's pause as she considered

this. Then a big smile spread across her face.

'Oh, you cheeky kiddies and your sweets!' she said, beaming. 'You go ahead and eat your treat. And help yourself to a spoonful of sticky toffee pudding too, there's enough to go around.'

'Nah, you're good,' I replied, and walked out without another word.

Umer and Wendy ran after me.

'Wow, that was easy,' said Umer, once we were back in the hall.

'I ain't messing around no more,' I replied. 'For a super-advanced race of evil masterminds, these aliens are pretty stupid when it comes to food. Just tell 'em what they want to hear.'

'So now what?' said Wendy.

'Do you have something we can play this on?'

'We could use my laptop,' she replied. 'It's at home.'

Linda Wang opened the door with a blue face pack on. She looked surprised to see us (though I guess that could have just been because she was blue).

'Uh-oh,' said Linda Wang, 'you three again. I don't want any more trouble from the police!'

'They're just here to use my computer,' replied

Wendy, marching past her and into the house.

'Thanks for coming to rescue Grandpa last night, Linda Wang,' I said, as I wiped my feet.

'Where is that old man now?' she asked. 'He looks like he should be in a care home.'

'Dunno,' I replied. 'He ran away from the police and we ain't seen him since. He'll be OK, I reckon. He's pretty smart, for an old guy.'

But, the truth was, I wasn't sure at all. Those aunties were everywhere and they'd be looking for him. He couldn't go home to his own house, that was for sure. Auntie Uzma would have him re-abducted before he could even get his slippers on.

We raced upstairs to Wendy's room, and she was opening the memory stick before I could even sit down.

'Ah, here we go,' she said, '"Badman Demo Clean".'

'That's it! That's the one!' I yelled.

'Why does it say "Clean"?' asked Umer, leaning in.

'Hmm . . .' said Wendy, opening the file. 'Hold up a minute . . .'

'What? What's wrong?' I asked.

'I'm just . . .' she replied, looking through the stacks of coloured bars that made up the track.

'There's bits missing. It's not all there. It's not like the last one.'

'Play it,' I told her.

Wendy hit PLAY and the familiar bass kicked in. It sounded all right so far. Then it just kept going. I waited for my first lines to start, but they never came.

'What's going on?' said Umer, looking puzzled.

'There are no vocals,' said Wendy and I at the same time.

'He must have removed them for you, like I did,' added Wendy.

'You kept saying you wanted to replace them,' said Umer. 'I guess he listened.'

'Right, OK, so we just need to record some more then, yeah?' I said.

'How?' replied Wendy. 'I don't have a microphone. Where did you do it last time?'

'School. Mr T set it up in the music room.'

'Somehow I don't think Mrs Jahib's going to help us with that,' added Umer.

Everyone was quiet for a time. I knew they were both thinking the same thing. There weren't really any other options.

'I'll do it,' I said.

'Really?' said Wendy. 'Live?'

I nodded.

'Are you sure?' said Umer. 'After . . . last time?'

'What choice do we have?'

'But it's our only shot,' said Wendy. 'If it was too much pressure before, this time it's going to be even worse! What if it goes wrong again? What if you –'

'I can do it,' I told her. 'It's different this time.'

And I truly hoped it was. Because Wendy was right: this *was* our one shot to pull this off. This wasn't about whether I was gonna be famous or not. This wasn't about me at all. This was about the end of the world.

It was a couple of hours later when I slid my house key into the door. I thought, if I was quiet enough, maybe I could just sneak upstairs to bed. Mum wouldn't care where I'd been, as long as I'd eaten. I wasn't keen on running into Dad though, especially after everything with the cricket team. He'd still be fuming.

I turned the key as quietly as I could and slipped inside. The smell of cooking was stronger than ever. I could hear Mum bashing pots and pans in the kitchen. Dad was nowhere to be seen.

I tiptoed up the stairs, trying not to make a sound. My only plan was to get into bed and practise my lyrics again and again. I had to get it right this time. I had to lock it down. No sign of Dad on the landing. His door was open but his bed was empty. He must be out. More confidently now, I walked across the hall and into my room.

He was sitting there on my bed, looking at his feet. He had a cricket ball in his hands and was turning it slowly in his fingers.

'Oh . . . hey, Dad,' I said, nearly jumping out of my skin.

'You have heard?' he said.

'About cricket?'

'It is over. Cancelled,' he replied, shaking his head.

'I'm sorry, Dad. I know how much you were enjoying it.'

'I asked you to do one thing for me,' he said, looking up. 'I asked you to play cricket and win. How is that so hard?'

'Dad . . .' I began, but he kept going.

'When I was your age, all I wanted to do was play cricket. I wish my father had wanted to play cricket with me.'

'I appreciate it, Dad, but it ain't me. I don't love cricket like you do.'

'You will!' he said, standing up.

'Eh?'

'You will keep practising. With me. Every day. And when you are ready we will beat that dog Siddiki and his worthless team of goats. You and me!'

'What, me and you against a whole cricket team? What are you talking about?'

'When I was your age, I thrashed eleven professional cricket players single-handedly at Gaddafi Stadium!'

'Dad! Stop!' I snapped. 'You didn't! No one's ever done that!'

'How dare you!' he shouted.

'Why you gotta do this all the time, man?'

'Right! That is it! You are grounded! You are not to leave this room!' he yelled, storming past me towards the door.

'What? You can't lock me in here – I've got school!'

'No more school! Your uncle in Karachi is *very* eager to give you proper Pakistani education.'

'You can't do this! I need to go in tomorrow!

I've got to do the talent show!'

'Talent show? Ha! There will be no talent show for you. You are finished at that school!'

'Dad!' I shouted, but it was too late.

He slammed the door shut. I heard the lock click. I tugged the handle with all my strength, but it was no good. I was trapped. A prisoner in my own house. And tomorrow, without me there, the aunties would finish everybody.

CHAPTER FOURTEEN
GROUNDED

I didn't think I'd be able to sleep at all that night, but I must have drifted off, because all of a sudden I woke with a start. Something was banging on my window.

'Humza! Open up!' came a familiar voice.

'Grandpa?' I whispered, a little too loudly.

Shh! he mouthed, from the other side of the glass. *Let me in.*

I jumped up and ran over, careful not to knock him off the roof as I pushed open the window.

'Grandpa, are you OK? What happened? You just vanished!'

'I'm fine,' he reassured me. 'I went for help.'

'Help? Who's gonna help us? It's a miracle you didn't get arrested last time.'

'Not the police,' he said, shaking his head. 'Real help.'

'Well, you better hurry up, because those slugs have got something big planned tomorrow. I think they're getting ready to finish it.'

'Tomorrow?' said Grandpa, looking concerned.

'Yeah, at the school talent show. That ship of theirs is parked up in the playground now. They're planning on holding the show there. Once they've got us where they want us – bang! They're gonna make their move. I just know it.'

Before Grandpa even had a chance to reply, we heard a voice from the hall.

'Humza?'

It was Mum! The key clicked in the lock, the handle turned and the door swung open. She was in her dressing gown, flour and icing sugar in her hair. Did she never sleep?

'Who are you talking to?' she said suspiciously.

I turned back to the window to find Grandpa had pulled his disappearing act.

'Uh . . . no one,' I replied, moving to sit back down on the bed. 'Just practising my lyrics for the talent show.'

I held up my notepad, so she could see the rap I'd written.

'Time for sleep,' she said as that grin – that weird, sinister grin my real mum would never make – spread across her face. 'It's a big day tomorrow,' she added. 'For both of us.'

'Both of us?' I replied.

'Did I not tell you? It is my first day of work,' she said, her smile widening. 'The school cannot run without a headmaster . . . or mistress.'

Her grin was the last thing to disappear in the shadows as she pulled the door closed behind her.

Whoa! . . . Mum was the new headmistress? This was bad. Those aliens were cunning enough already. Imagine what they'd be like with someone as ingenious as my mum in charge!

When I returned to the window, I wasn't surprised to find the garden empty and Grandpa gone.

After that, I could barely sleep. I tossed and turned for the rest of the night, just waiting for morning to arrive. But when it did, it turned out I wasn't going anywhere. Dad kept me locked in the room the whole of the next day. I was his prisoner. Completely stuck. Hours passed. I couldn't even get to the phone to let Umer know what had happened. They'd be thinking the aunties had got me. It was a nightmare.

Eventually, to keep from going stir crazy, I started reading the old PIA comics I'd drawn. I'd found a big pile of them in my drawer while looking for something I might use as a grappling hook. They were pretty good, and it was helping to take my mind off the fact that the world was about to end.

I'd just finished reading one about the PIA's top operative, Agent Khan. He'd been infiltrating the headquarters of a villainous chicken-shop boss. He was like an evil version of the KFC Colonel, and he'd been swapping chicken out for rat meat. In the end he gets punched out by Agent Khan and falls into a vat of secret sauce. Then Khan says, 'Finger-lickin' dead.'

You gotta admit that's pretty sick. That's Hollywood-level writing, and I was only, like, eight when I did it. If it wasn't for this alien invasion and the world coming to an end, I was pretty sure that, one day, they'd have made a film adaptation. I sat looking at my drawings of Agent Khan and daydreaming about who they might have cast.

Huh . . . That's weird . . .

I had never noticed it before, but Agent Khan did look like someone. In fact, he looked so much like them, I couldn't believe I'd never spotted it. Agent Khan was the spitting image of Grandpa. Not now, obviously, but when he was much younger. My dad had shown me some old photos of him once as a joke, laughing at the idea that Grandpa was ever a young man. And, I swear, it could have been Agent Khan. How had I never spotted it before?

I started flipping back through all the old comics, looking for one panel in particular. I was sure that early on, when I'd just started drawing them, I had put in a few more details about our mysterious hero. Something was telling me I needed to remember.

There it was, the page I was looking for: Agent Khan imprisoned in Professor Pig's underwater lair. (Don't ask me why a pig has an underwater lair. I was eight.) Locked in his cell, Khan had no chance of escaping. Professor Pig was so certain of his victory he'd had a tombstone carved.

HERE LIES TARIQ KHAN – WHO DIED OF BEING A BIG, FAT, STUPID, SMELLY IDIOT

HOW DO YOU LIKE IT, KHAN? I COULDN'T RESIST.

'Tariq Khan . . .' I said, lowering the page.

I pictured all the 'Tariq' boxes in Grandpa's loft. Had he been my inspiration for Agent Khan all along? Why on earth had I picked Grandpa? And how had I forgotten? Sure, Grandpa was starting to seem more interesting lately but most of the time I'd known him he'd been pretty much a zombie. Why would I use him for a comic-book hero?

It made me smile though. I guess, whether I'd been aware of it or not, I must have always liked Grandpa. I turned back to the comic to see how Grandpa would escape. As I scanned the page, the story began to come back to me. My mouth fell open. This was it! I remembered this one! I remembered how he got out! This was the answer!

In the comic, Agent Khan had used his trusty secret agent's gadget pen to push the key out of the lock, on to a sheet of paper. He'd slid the paper back into the room . . . and the key had come with it.

In an instant, I was crouching by the door, a pen in one hand and the comic in the other. Just like in the story, I slid the comic under the gap, then wiggled the pen about in the lock until the key started to jiggle. It had to be just right. If I pushed too hard, the key would bounce off down the hallway and I'd never get it back. I applied a little more pressure as I wiggled the pen back and forth. All at once, the key slipped free, and I heard it drop on the other side.

Very carefully, I slid the comic back into the room. The key was lying right on the edge of the page. I had it.

I was out of my bedroom and running for the front door before I could even do my laces. I heard a crash from the living room.

'Humza?' shouted my dad.

I heard a plate smashing on the ground. He must have spilled whatever he was in the middle of eating.

I grabbed the door handle and tore it open, just in time to see Dad burst out of the living room. He crashed into the hallway wall, taking out a table lamp and a photo of my mum at the beach. His vest was covered in curry sauce from his spilled dinner and his pyjama bottoms weren't tied, so he was having to hold them up with one hand. He growled at me as our eyes locked. There was a moment's pause. And then he charged.

His foot had become tangled in the telephone

cable and he tore it out of the wall as he stumbled forward. I wasn't about to stick around to watch though. I leapt over the gate and tore off down the street. When I got to the corner, I stole a quick glance back. He was still coming. His face was dark red. He had a weird look in his eye that was either determination or a small stroke. This wasn't over yet. I ran for the park.

It was two minutes from the house, and I hoped I might be able to lose him in the wooded section, or maybe among the hedges near the playground. As I sprinted through the park gates he came hurtling round the corner and crashed into a parked van, setting off its alarm. But it wasn't going to slow him down. His eyes narrowed when he saw me and, in an instant, he was off again.

Through the park we ran. Young mums and their confused toddlers watched us tear past. We were both in pretty bad shape and were dripping with sweat by that point. I started to worry that if my dad didn't kill me, the exercise would almost certainly kill *him*. But he wasn't giving up.

He managed to stick behind me all the way through the woods. I tell you, he was nimble on his feet for a fat guy holding up his trousers. Even in the hedges, no matter what I tried – ducking and diving, weaving and hiding – I just couldn't seem to lose him. He tore through bushes like they were made of paper. He looked like King Kong crashing through the jungle.

I was just starting to worry that I might have to give up and try to reason with him when I remembered the pond. If I could lead Dad to the middle of it, I knew we'd both be forced to run across the stepping stones. I'd done it a thousand times. I could probably do it blindfold. I could definitely do it at a sprint. But could he? It was my only chance.

As I weaved around the last bush, gasping for air, I spotted it up ahead – the long, snaking pond. It stretched off in either direction as far as the eye could see. If you didn't know better, you'd have thought it was a river. There were a dozen or so stepping stones, right in the middle, that cut right the way across it. Kids had stuck 'em there years ago so they didn't have to go the long way round. And beyond the stones was the exit.

I didn't hesitate – I just leapt. If it had rained recently the stones would be slippery. Landing on a wet stone at this speed would send me in head first, guaranteed.

But my foot found its grip and I sprang forward towards the next stone. Then the next. I didn't slow down for a second. I leapt two a time at one point. Before I knew it I was on the other bank. I couldn't help myself; I turned back to watch. My dad had come to a stop. He looked left, trying to figure out how far he'd have to go around. He looked right. He realized he had no choice.

He stepped on to the first stone. They were pretty small, even for my feet. For Dad, this wasn't going to be easy.

'Just go back!' I shouted.

'Never!' he cried, stepping to the next stone.

'Dad! I have to go! I have to do this!'

'You will do as you are told!'

He was approaching the halfway mark when he began to wobble badly.

'Dad, go back while you can!'

'I am not going back!' he yelled. 'I am going to punish you worse than you have ever been punished in your life!'

But the more he yelled, the wobblier he got.

'Dad! You're not gonna make it!'

'I am!' he cried, balancing on one leg.

He was swaying all over the place now. While one of his hands was kept busy stopping his pyjama bottoms from falling down, the other one was waving this way and that in an effort to keep himself from toppling in.

'Dad, please . . .' I yelled, but it was too late.

As he began to lose his balance, the hand holding up his pyjama bottoms shot out instinctively to try and catch hold of something. But, now, there was nothing left to keep his great baggy pyjamas from slipping down to his knees. In an instant they were tangled round his feet, preventing him from raising his legs properly. His grubby white pants, with the fraying elastic and the holes around the bum, were exposed to everybody. I saw a young mum cover her toddler's eyes.

'Humzz-aaaarrrggghhhh!' he cried.

Everything seemed to go into slow motion as he finally lost all balance and tipped over into the pond. I should have run straight away, but I couldn't leave him. Not like that, upside down in a duck pond with his bum out. Thankfully, he popped back up a moment later with some pondweed on his head.

His teeth were gritted. His eyes were burning. He was nuclear.

'Dad,' I said in as calm a voice as I could manage, 'I have to do this. You don't have to believe me, but, I swear, I'm telling the truth. These aunties are aliens. Mum's an alien. And by tonight all of us are gonna be aliens! I *have* to try and stop them!'

He stared at me with red, bulging eyes. There was so much water dribbling down his face from the pondweed that I thought he might be crying.

'Aliens? Aliens?' he yelled. 'Do you think I am simple-minded like Grandpa?'

'Grandpa ain't simple-minded – he's the one who figured this all out!'

'He is a joke!' shouted my dad. 'He has wasted his life!'

'No he hasn't! He's happier than you are! He doesn't need to lie about everything. He doesn't need to impress people so he can feel good about himself. All my life, you've been telling me how great you are. How many amazing things you did growing up in Pakistan. And you know what I realized? I'm doing exactly the same thing! I go around telling everyone I'm gonna be a superstar. I make stuff up just to sound important. And none of it's real. It's just about being scared. Scared of not being special. Not being liked. Not being good enough.'

Dad wasn't moving now. He was just stood in the middle of the pond watching me.

'But you know what?' I told him. 'Truth is, you never had to do any of that. Not with me. You're my dad. I was born thinking you were great. You came to a new country, made a business from nothing, bought your own house and a whole load of toilets. Yeah, it ain't gangsta, but it's pretty amazing. I don't need you to have punched a bear or jumped over a Burger King. Because that other stuff you did, the stuff you *don't* boast about – that stuff's pretty amazing already.'

Dad just stared at me. He didn't look angry any more. He had an expression on his face I'd never seen before. I still don't know what you'd call it.

'I've got something important to do, Abu-jee. I know you'll be angry and I know you'll punish me, but I need to do this. You don't have to believe me about the aliens. You don't have to help me. But, I swear, that *ain't* Mum. And it ain't Auntie Uzma. And tonight, if I don't stop 'em, they're gonna take over everything. So I've got to go.'

And I ran. Out of the park and towards the setting sun. Towards the school.

CHAPTER FIFTEEN
THE TALENT SHOW

Nicholas Gemmel was practising a pretty weird dance routine as I ran through the school gates.

'Have I missed it?' I yelled.

'Aargh!' screeched Nicholas, dropping his coloured handkerchiefs and flinching as if I was gonna attack him.

'Damn it, Nick! The talent show – is it over?' I shouted.

'No. It's on right now,' he replied, picking up his hankies. 'You don't need to shout at me.'

'Sorry,' I said, turning to run, before skidding to a stop immediately.

'Nick,' I called, looking back at him. 'Go home, man. Seriously.'

I didn't wait to see if he listened. There was no time. I ran across the playground and over to where the sports field had sat just two days earlier. The new canteen towered above everything: bright glass and polished steel. It was an evil canteen if ever I'd seen one.

'Humza!' shouted Wendy from the doorway. 'Where have you been?'

'Doesn't matter . . . I'm here now,' I said, gasping for breath.

'Is Umer with you?'

'Umer?' I said, confused. 'No? He's with you, isn't he?'

'When you didn't come in, he went looking for you. He never came back.'

'You don't think . . .' I began.

'I don't know,' replied Wendy.

Neither of us said anything for a moment. It didn't bear thinking about.

'He'll come back,' I murmured. 'He has to.'

'Yeah,' agreed Wendy. 'He'll come back.'

She didn't sound convinced. Neither did I.

'Are we ready to go?' I asked.

'Uh-huh. We're all hooked up to the sound system. But, Humza, there's something you've got to see.'

Wendy led me inside, through the great dark

metal doors of the new canteen. We were in a long, well-lit corridor. It felt kinda like it had last time round, but, like the outside of the building, they'd adapted it. Tweaked it. It felt like a school hallway, sure, but not a normal one. It was too cold, too hard. I felt like I was being watched.

Somewhere up ahead, I could hear music playing. My heart was thumping in my chest. We were back on their territory. Nothing in here was safe.

'Look,' said Wendy, as we arrived at an inner set of doors.

With great care not to make a sound, Wendy pushed them open a crack and gestured for me to look in. Even though it was dark inside, I knew immediately it was the same room we'd been in before: the huge open warehouse. They'd reconfigured it all to look like a canteen, and at the front they'd set up a large stage for the show. Amanda Mump from Year Five was standing in the spotlight singing a song about cats.

'Scary, huh?' said Wendy.

'The cat song?' I replied.

'No, look,' said Wendy, pointing. 'The audience.'

I hadn't even looked at the audience – hundreds

of people, adults and children, all facing the stage. It was pretty dark, so it took me a minute to work out what I was seeing. And then it hit me. Every single grown-up in the room was wearing the same grin – they all had that same look in their eyes. And it wasn't just the aunties; it was everyone we'd seen at the warehouse. All the missing teachers. All the missing adults. They were awake now. And all of them were slug people.

I pulled my head back into the corridor.

'It's everyone!' I said.

'Yeah,' said Wendy. 'Mr Turnbull's in there. And the headmaster. Loads of people I've never even seen before. The only ones in that audience who aren't slugs already are the kids. And they're next.'

'Not if we've got anything to say about it,' I replied. 'Come on.'

We made our way past rows of seats, to the side of the stage. No one seemed to notice us as we slipped behind the curtain. A small set of stairs led up to where Wendy had hooked her computer into the PA system. Mr T's memory stick was poking out the side. Everything looked ready to go.

'Ah, Humza! Good,' said Mrs Masood, appearing from the shadows, clipboard in hand. 'You are up next. Once you are finished, take a bow and head out through the little red door.'

She pointed to the far side of the stage, where I could just make out a small red doorway. Wendy leaned in close to my ear.

'Everyone who's performed has gone through that door,' she whispered. 'I haven't seen them since.'

It was happening. It was happening right now. Somewhere in this canteen–spaceship, the aunties were turning kids into slug people.

'I'm ready,' I said to Wendy.

She nodded, smiling.

'I know you are. You've got this,' she replied.

'I don't think Umer's gonna come,' I told her. 'You're gonna have to play me in.'

Wendy nodded.

'It'll be OK,' she said, putting one hand on my arm. 'We'll find him.'

'That won't be necessary,' came a voice from behind me . . . my mum's voice. 'We found him already.'

I turned to see Umer standing opposite us, in the shadows. On either side of him were Auntie Uzma and my mum.

'Umer!' I cried. 'Are you all right?'

'Of course,' said Umer in a calm voice. 'I'm better than ever.'

As he stepped forward, the light from the stage fell across his face, revealing that grin: wide and wild and cruel. Umer was gone. They'd taken him.

'Step away from the laptop, Wendy,' he said. 'I'll take over from here.'

'Umer's told us everything,' added my mother.

'It's over now,' said my auntie.

Umer took another step towards Wendy.

'It's going to be OK,' he said, reaching out towards the memory stick.

They knew. They knew everything that Umer knew. They knew about the plan. The song. The memory stick. I felt sick at the realization.

The audience began to clap. Amanda's song had finished. The rhythmic clapping got louder and louder. Umer took another step towards us. Amanda walked through the little red door at the side of the stage. My mum and my auntie grinned. This was the end.

'I'm sorry, Umer,' I said.

He only had time to look up from the computer for an instant before I shoved him with all my strength. He was bigger than me, but the surprise of it caught him off guard and knocked him backwards. He stumbled, crashing into my mum and auntie. It wouldn't stop him for long, but it bought me enough time to make a grab for the memory stick.

I tore it out of the machine and ran out on to the stage. The clapping stopped instantly. I turned to face the audience. The aliens. They all smiled at once. I will never forget how creepy that looked. The students among them were beginning to look suspicious that something wasn't right. But they couldn't know what we knew. They had no idea what was about to happen to them.

When I looked back, my mum, Auntie Uzma and Umer were all walking towards me.

'It's over, Humza,' said my mum. 'Give Umer the memory stick and go through the door.'

Umer held out his hand as he walked towards me. How could we fight them when Umer knew everything I did? He knew everywhere I'd run to, everywhere I'd hide. He probably knew what I was thinking before I'd even thought it. And then it hit me. There was one thing Umer didn't know. One thing he couldn't know. Because I'd promised never to tell anyone.

'Ladies, gentlemen and alien parasites!' I shouted, turning to the audience.

Umer stopped briefly in his tracks, a confused look on his face.

'Behold, a regular 128-gigabyte memory stick!'

I held out the stick for them all to see. I closed my other hand around it.

'Humza . . .' said my mother, her eyes narrowing. 'What are you doing?'

'Magic,' I said to her, and then blew hard on my closed hand.

I whipped open my fingers to reveal that the memory stick had vanished. The whole room gasped. Umer took a step back. I guess alien slugs don't have sleight of hand where they come from. You probably need hands for that.

'How . . . ?' gasped Umer. 'Where . . . ?'

'What have you done?' cried my mother.

'Where is it?' shouted Auntie Uzma.

'Maybe you should check your pockets,' I replied.

'Quickly!' screamed my mother. 'Search your pockets! We must find it!'

The three of them began to tear through their pockets, looking for the missing memory stick – but it was nowhere to be found. And that's cos it was back in Wendy's hand, who was already plugging it into the computer.

That brief moment of misdirection, as they searched their pockets, was all I needed to throw the memory stick back to Wendy. She'd plugged it in and hit PLAY. The beat dropped like a ton of thunder.

'Humza!' shouted Wendy, and she hurled something through the darkness. I couldn't even see what it was, as it flipped towards me through the air, soaring over Mum and Uzma's heads.

I jumped up to grab it. The microphone slapped into my palm. My fingers closed round it. My dad would have been proud – it was a hell of a catch.

Umer's expression dropped. He could see what was happening. My mum, my auntie, every slug in the audience – they all suddenly knew. I lifted the mic to my lips, turned to face them, and . . .

NOTHING.

I couldn't remember a word. I was blank. It was happening all over again. I had no idea how the song started.

'Come on!' shouted Wendy, but it was no good.

I lowered the mic. Umer, or at least the slug controlling Umer, stopped moving towards me. A smile spread across his face. He began to laugh. He knew. He knew I didn't have the lyrics. He knew I was blank.

Behind him, my mum began to laugh. Then Auntie Uzma. Then every single slug person in the hall. They all began to laugh at once. The noise of it grew louder and louder and louder. It was the worst thing I'd ever heard.

And then there came a *boom* from the back of the hall. Someone had kicked the double doors open. The laughter stopped in an instant as everyone turned to look. Though the room was dark, the lights from the corridor lit him up like a Christmas tree. He was dressed in his cricket whites. He was carrying half a dozen cricket bats under each arm. He looked me straight in the eye.

'You may be lying,' shouted my dad, 'or you may be telling the truth. It does not matter. I believe you.'

A smile spread across his face. And not a freaky sinister alien smile but the smile I'd known since I was a kid. The smile he wore when we stayed up late together to watch wrestling. The smile he wore when we had ice cream for dinner after Eid. The smile he wore when Pakistan won the cricket.

'So where are these aliens we are fighting, huh?' he said.

And that was it. The fog in my mind suddenly lifted. A single word popped into my head. It wasn't much, but it was enough. I knew how to start.

Umer saw it in my face. I saw it in his. But he was too late. Before he could take those last few steps to reach me, I had already begun. The words started to flow . . .

'B to the A to the D to the Man,
Ain't gonna stand for no alien plan.
You mess with my school
        and you mess with my fam,
So now I'm hitting back with my lyrical jam.

'Light years beyond anything that you've heard,
T drops the beat, Badman freestyles the words.
You should've left town, cos your plan is absurd,
But now it's too late – you're about to get served.'

The effect was immediate. All over the room, teachers, dinner ladies, audience members began to fall to their knees and retch. And right in front of me on the stage, just a couple of feet away, so did Umer. It was working! I had to keep going! Even now, I ain't got a clue where the words were coming from. It was like I was speaking faster than I could think. All I knew was that I couldn't stop. Not yet!

'You made a mistake when you thought
**   I would freeze.**
I'm stinging like a billion pencil-case bees.
It's one thing to mess with a man's auntie,
But no one gets to mess with my Umer but me.

'Pushed us too far, now you're in a tight spot.
Wanna rule the world?
**   Well you just blew your shot!**
You think you can touch me, I'm much too hot.
You look like a bin bag filled up with snot.'

The slugs were everywhere now, spilling on to the floor, rolling about with big, wide, panicked eyes. It was working! But I wasn't done yet. I had to keep going until every last slug was out.

'Feeding us up till we're ready to burst?
Your plan or your looks,
          I ain't sure which is worse.
Mess with my mum and you'll leave in a hearse.
Is he nearly done? Nah, I got another verse.

'Green space-slugs made a judgement of error,
Messed with our school –
          now you tremble in terror.
Thought you could beat us? We've already won!
That's right, drop the mic, yeah – Badman done.'

Right on cue, just as my mic hit the ground, Wendy brought up the house lights. The full scale of the chaos was revealed.

Damn . . .

The song had done its job. There were giant green slugs everywhere. Big white eyeballs flashed about in panic. The adults who had been slug hosts were all still too stunned and confused to act. Most of them were still on their hands and knees, or slouched in their seats.

But the kids were alert. This is the kind of thing kids are prepared for. You think when we're playing battle games that it's just for fun? You think

worrying about monsters under the bed for years doesn't equip you for fighting 'em? Trust me, it does. And it was slug-fighting time.

And let's not forget my dad. If ever there was a big kid who could rise to a challenge like this, it was him. I could see him at the front of the audience rallying the cricket team. As the lads ran towards him, he started dishing out the bats he was carrying. He threw the first to Jamal Jones. Jamal caught it in one hand and wheeled round to face a group of slugs heading straight towards him. Crack! He sent them flying across the room.

'Six!' cheered my dad.

He dished out the rest of the bats, keeping two for

himself, one in each hand. I saw him windmilling along, knocking slugs this way and that. He was having the time of his life.

Now don't get me wrong: not every kid's built for fighting alien slugs. But every kid rose to the challenge in one way or another. Wendy began organizing the evacuation, two kids to an adult, leading them towards the main doors.

I turned round to see if Dad had made it to Mum, but he was on the far side of the room twisting an enormous space-slug between his two fists like he was wringing a towel. He flung it on to the stage and picked up his cricket bats.

'Dad!' I shouted, but he couldn't hear me over the din.

Just then, something whipped over my head, missing me by millimetres as I ducked to avoid it. It was one of the glass tubes from the warehouse. It looked like they weren't just good for doughnut feeding – now they were attacking us. I saw one tube crash into the cricket team, sending them flying like skittles. Another one was whipping around the room, sucking up slugs one at a time. They wriggled into the mouth of the pipe – squidging and stretching their fat little bodies to fit – before they vanished upwards with a slurp, sucked away into the darkness overhead. They were escaping!

I spotted Mum, on her hands and knees beside the stage, looking pretty shell-shocked. Nearby, I watched as Umer lost his balance and stumbled into a row of empty chairs, but no one helped him. Down the hallway, Wendy was trying to lead the evacuation, but it was chaos and no one was moving fast enough. The corridor was blocked with people trying to get out. This wasn't over yet.

I ran towards the exit. If we couldn't start clearing a path outside, we couldn't help anyone. Pushing through the crowd, I found Wendy near the front, supporting Mr Turnbull. I ducked under Mr T's free arm and took as much of his weight as I could. The exit to the playground was just twenty feet away now.

'Come on, sir – we're nearly there,' I said, but Mr T was out of it.

Man, I tell you, dragging an unconscious adult is harder than it looks. I glanced behind me to see how the rest of the kids were managing. Two or three of them were supporting each grown-up (four or five when it came to some of the bigger aunties).

They were struggling as much as we were. This was going to take all night! The slugs were everywhere. It wouldn't be long before they regrouped and started fighting back. We had to move faster.

There were just a few feet left to the exit, but my legs already felt like they might give out.

'Sir, you've got to walk!' I cried, and, as I said it, I buckled.

My legs went from underneath me and I stumbled forward, pulling Wendy and Mr T down. We'd have hit the ground if it hadn't been for the giant.

Now, I've seen some pretty big Pakistani guys in movies and stuff, but this was by far the biggest. He was dressed entirely in black army gear, with shoulders like minivans and a jaw like a skip. He caught Mr T in one huge fist and hoisted him on to his back.

Before I could even pick myself up and ask who the hell he was, a blinding light exploded from the playground. What was going on? I couldn't see a thing. I felt someone grab me, pulling me to my feet. It definitely wasn't Wendy. Whoever had hold of me wouldn't let go. I struggled to get free, kicking and squirming. The arms pulled me tighter. Wait . . . Was this a hug?

'Humza! Stop! It's me!' said a voice, close to my ear.

'Grandpa?' I shouted.

I grabbed him and hugged him back. As my eyes adjusted to the light, I saw that he wasn't alone. There were loads more of the soldier-looking guys in black, piling out of trucks and pouring into the building behind him. Every one of them looked like some kind of Pakistani GI Joe.

'Who the hell are these guys?' I asked.

'Explain later,' he said. 'Evacuate first.'

The soldier guys began to stream into the building to help the kids who were escorting the adults.

'Wendy!' I shouted. 'I'm going back for the others. Are you OK?'

'Yeah, we'll be fine. Go,' she said, before turning to help another of the teachers out into the night.

I ran back into the hall, with Grandpa close behind me.

'Where is Uzma?' he yelled.

I scanned the room. It was carnage. Fighting, running, shouting. Then I spotted her.

'There!' I said, pointing to Auntie Uzma, who was looking dazed beside the stage. 'She ain't one of them no more. Get her out of here. I'm going after Mum.'

Grandpa nodded and disappeared into the chaos. And it *was* chaos. There were slugs squealing and squelching in every direction. There were dazed grown-ups wandering about like overfed zombies. Everywhere you turned, kids were battling glass tubes and alien monsters with whatever weapons they could lay their hands on – chairs, school bags, shoes.

And right there, in the middle of it all, was my dad, swinging two cricket bats at once as he cleared a path towards my mum.

'Dad!' I shouted.

'Hello, boy!' he called back, a big grin on his face. It was amazing. He was having a good time!

'Here!' he yelled, and threw me one of the bats.

'Thanks!' I said, catching it just in time to clobber a glass tube that was racing towards Erika Yurp – who was busy pummelling a slug with one of her plimsolls.

The tube reeled off into the darkness and vanished out of sight.

'Good shot!' shouted my dad, before walloping a fat green slug across the room and on to the far side of the stage.

'You too!' I yelled.

'I told you: in your genes!' he said, and he laughed.

We were both grinning now. Mum was just a few feet away. We were winning.

And that's when the floor began to shake. Not just shake. To rumble, violently. Like an earthquake. I can tell you this now: we do not get a lot of earthquakes in Eggington. In fact, I'm pretty sure we get none. This could mean only one thing.

'The ship's taking off!' I shouted. 'We gotta get out of here!'

Dad nodded, and without another word he swung his bat, clearing six slugs at once. We dived forward and grabbed hold of Mum, each taking her by an arm.

'Humza? Mohammed?' she said, raising her head to look at us. 'Where are we?'

'Hey, Mum, welcome back! We'll explain everything later. But, for now, we need to get the hell out of here.'

She nodded and let us help her towards the exit. The mysterious army guys were doing a great job clearing the place, but even they realized something was wrong when the rumbling had started. They began evacuating fast. I saw Grandpa and Uzma making their way out ahead of us. I saw six soldiers staggering under the weight of Mr Offalbox as they dragged him towards the exit. As we got to the double doors, I glanced back into the hall to check for stragglers. The room looked clear. We were the last.

And that's when I spotted him.

Amid the chaos, the upturned chairs and the battered slugs, Umer was lying face down. You could barely see him, he was so covered in debris. The last of the army guys was running for the exit.

'Hey!' I shouted.

'Get out of here, now!' said the soldier in a strong Pakistani accent, before heading out with a dinner lady over each shoulder.

'But – my friend!' I shouted after him.

It was no good. They were leaving.

'Dad!' I yelled. 'Take Mum. I'll be right behind you.'

'What?' he snapped, looking angry and scared all at once.

'I'll be OK, I promise. Go!'

I didn't stay to hear his protest. I let go of Mum's arm and ran back into the hall. Getting over all the upturned chairs was hard enough but with the building shaking like this it was next to impossible. I wheeled the cricket bat around just in time to knock a feeding tube out before it tackled me. A pair of slugs leapt at me, and I sent them flying into a stack of chairs.

Umer was only a few feet away now. But it looked like the glass tubes had found him too. A pair of them had slipped under his arms and were dragging him towards the door on the stage.

'Hey!' I shouted, leaping on to an upturned chair and firing myself towards them. 'That's my Umer!'

I smashed the bat into the first of the tubes with

everything I had. Whatever it was made of, it was already clearly starting to give, with cracks running up and down it. When I connected, it exploded into a million pieces. The bat slammed into the second tube, and, though it didn't shatter, it was enough to knock Umer loose.

I fell on to him with a crash, as shards of glass rained down on us. Umer stirred and opened his eyes.

'Hey, Humza,' he said with a dazed smile.

'Man, you owe me big for this,' I said, pulling myself up. 'Now, come on! We gotta get out of here.'

I helped Umer to his feet and we started heading towards the door. By this point, most of the slugs were looking more battered than Umer and they weren't putting up a fight any more. Even the tubes left us alone.

Yeah, that's right, I thought. *You've met your match, haven't you?*

Turns out, though, they knew something we didn't. As we approached the main doors, I realized what it was: they weren't trying to stop us because they didn't need to. The ship had already begun to take off. Where the playground used to be, now there was just a drop. And it was getting bigger every second.

'Humza!' shouted my dad, ten feet below. 'Jump! You have to jump!'

'Jump!' shouted Wendy.

'We'll catch you!' shouted Grandpa.

I looked at Umer. He was still half asleep.

'Man, I hope you never have to do this for me,' I told him.

Then I shoved him out the door and into the night sky. I didn't have time to watch him land. We were getting higher and higher every moment.

I closed my eyes . . . and leapt.

And that's how I died. The End.

Nah, not really. Course I didn't die! How would I have written all this if I'd died? Don't be stupid. I'm fine! I broke my arm, but whatever. Broken arm's gangsta.

The last thing I remember before blacking out was the school canteen floating above me in the night sky. It hovered over the crowd for just a moment. And then, with a flash of light, it was gone, firing off into the stars above.

CHAPTER SIXTEEN
BADMAN DONE

I thought nothing would ever be the same again after that. I mean, how could it be? There were aliens out there! Plus, we'd just saved the world. We were gonna be the most famous kids on the planet, right? Nope. Apparently, Grandpa's friends had other ideas. And before you start asking me who the hell these friends of Grandpa's were who showed up with an army, I'm just about to tell you.

Funny thing is, the clues were there all along, I just didn't put it together. Sure, the last few months had taught me that Grandpa kept a few tricks up his sleeve, but this last one I don't think I could ever have guessed. See, it turns out my comics about the secret agents of the PIA hadn't entirely come from my imagination after all. Though the real guys go by a different name ...

'You do not remember?' asked Grandpa, as we sat together in the doctor's waiting room.

'Nah, not really,' I replied, trying to scratch the skin under my plaster with a pencil.

Man, I was glad to be getting this thing off. A month of not being able to scratch an itch is almost worse than an alien invasion.

'I guess I kind of remember you telling me stories as a kid,' I said. 'I remember sitting on your knee.'

'You were the only one I could tell,' he said. 'Like the magic tricks, those stories were secret. You were so little. You would not tell anyone. You liked my stories.'

'I guess I must have. I've been drawing comics about you for years. I just didn't realize it. I thought I made 'em up.'

Grandpa laughed.

'I had no idea,' he said, shaking his head. 'You never showed me.'

'I can't believe you're a spy, man. I can't believe the PIA are real and you're one of them.'

'Not "PIA",' said Grandpa. 'We are called the Agency. And, anyway, I am retired now.'

'Yeah? You didn't look so retired when you showed up with the cavalry last month.'

Grandpa shrugged and gave a small smile. He was quiet for a moment. He looked like he was remembering something from a long time ago.

'Hey,' I eventually said, 'cos you're always sleeping, does that make you a sleeper agent?'

'Not funny,' he replied, grinning. 'You try doing two jobs. Dry cleaner's all day, secret Agency all night. Very tiring.'

'Yeah, I bet. Still, it was a pretty good disguise. I don't think I'd have ever figured you for a spy.'

'Not a spy. Agent.'

'What's the difference?'

'We have many different roles. Far more than just spying. Work with many different agencies, all over the globe.'

'Huh. Maybe I've underestimated things in Pakistan a bit.'

'There will be time to put that right,' he said with a smile.

'Does anyone else in the family know about all this?'

'No.'

'Not even Auntie Uzma?'

'Especially not Auntie Uzma. Oh boy, she would make nihari out of me if she found out what I have been up to all these years.'

'Damn, Grandpa, you are a sly old goat.'

'Simple misdirection,' he said, slipping a coin from his pocket. 'Like magic tricks. Make people notice one thing . . .'

He flipped the coin towards me, high into the air, and I caught it as it fell.

'. . . so they fail to notice another,' he added.

When I turned back to him, Grandpa was holding a red gift-wrapped box in his lap. It had appeared from nowhere in the split second my eye was turned.

'What's that?' I asked him.

'Your reward,' he said, passing it to me. 'For saving the world, for saving your family and, most importantly, for finishing your first-ever after-school job.'

'Ah, man, you didn't have to get me anything.'

'I was glad to have spent time with you again. Go on!' He grinned, nodding to the box. 'Open it.'

I peeled back the wrapping paper at the top. I didn't even need to open it all the way to work out what it was. White moulded plastic with sharp

black outlining! Optical zoom lens! 16-megapixel
sensor!

'The Matsani S3000 Home Pro Compact Video
Camera!' I yelled.

Grandpa laughed.

'So next time you need to prove an alien
invasion, you are ready to go,' he added.

'Yeah, this would have been pretty helpful a
month ago,' I said, peeling off the rest of the paper.
'Thanks, Grandpa. You didn't have to do this.'

'You've earned it,' he said, smiling.

'Grandpa,' I said, looking up, 'I still don't
understand why we can't talk about what happened.

Why cover it up? Aliens tried to take over the world. It's big news.'

'People are not ready yet. Maybe one day. But, for now, the Agency says no. People get scared. People panic. So they cover things up. And life goes on.'

'But I still don't understand how they made everyone forget what happened,' I said. 'How'd they do that? Mind control? Hypnosis? Some kind of brain-melting ray gun?'

'Honestly, I do not know. They don't tell me everything,' replied Grandpa. 'But at least you and your friends get to remember. That will have to do.'

'Yeah, I guess. Thanks for convincing them not to wipe our memories too.'

'Oh, I did not have to convince them,' replied Grandpa. 'They want to meet you.'

'Who, the Agency?'

'Mm-hmm.' Grandpa nodded.

'They want to meet me? Really? When?'

'Humza Khan,' called the nurse.

'Right now,' replied Grandpa with a grin.

Leaving the camera on my chair, I followed the nurse down the corridor to Doctor Kapoor's room. But, when she opened the door, it wasn't him there waiting for me as usual. Instead, there were two gigantic soldier-looking guys in the little room, standing hunched over, arms folded. They were crammed into dark suits and neither of them had taken off their sunglasses, even though we were inside. Gangsta.

Sitting between them, behind Doctor Kapoor's desk, was a third guy. He was normal-sized, not wearing sunglasses, and he smiled at me when I entered.

'Hello, Humza,' said the desk guy in a strong Pakistani accent. 'Come, come, come,' he added, gesturing to the seat opposite. 'We have much to talk about . . .'

∗

A week later, Umer, Wendy and I were in Mr Turnbull's classroom, adding the last touches to the music video. The Matsani S3000 sat on the desk, plugged into Wendy's laptop. Wendy was doing the editing, as she was the only one who'd figured out how to use it. Umer and I were behind her, giving her direction.

'Looking good,' said Mr Turnbull as he walked past, carrying a stack of sheet music. 'You can have ten more minutes, then you're going to have to get out into that sunshine. It's your last break time ever, guys. Go and enjoy it.'

'Last one at *this* school,' I replied. 'But it all starts again in September. I wish you were coming with us, sir.'

'Well, you know where I am if you ever need me,' he said with a smile. 'I'm just glad I was able to help you finish your track. I think you might have something special there.'

Umer, Wendy and I all shot each other a quick glance. Mr T had no idea how 'special' his track was, how important it had been. He had no memory of the aliens, of the abduction, of the rescue.

It had all been wiped. It was like none of it had ever happened. And who'd believe us if we told them?

When the final bell sounded, every kid in the school ran through the gates cheering. And none of them cheered as loud or as long as the Year Sixes. Primary school was done. We had the whole summer ahead of us. I had the finished music video on a memory stick in my bag and I was with my two best friends. Life was pretty good.

'It's still so weird that we can't talk to anyone about it, isn't it?' said Umer as we walked into the park.

'Yeah, I reckon it'll probably feel weird for a while,' I replied. 'Maybe forever.'

'Why do you think they let us remember?' asked Wendy. 'I mean, why just us?'

Man, I was so desperate to tell my friends about my meeting at the doctor's with the Agency guys. But they'd made me promise to keep that a secret too. Damn, these secret agents sure can be secretive. This was gonna be the hardest thing I'd ever done.

'I guess it's a reward,' I said. 'You know, for saving the whole planet.'

We walked quietly through the park, towards the pond.

'Are you going to put it online?' said Umer, after a while.

'The music video?' I replied. 'I guess so. I haven't really thought about it.'

It was funny – I still loved working on the track, writing the rap lyrics, shooting the video, all of it. But what I realized now was that just making it was the important bit. If you're lucky enough to get that excited about doing something, then what happens to it afterwards really isn't that big a deal.

Putting too much pressure on yourself over what's going to happen next can stop you enjoying what's happening right now. And what's the point of that? I'd got so caught up in the idea of being famous that I couldn't even perform properly when I got the chance.

So, as I stood there looking at the stepping stones across the pond, I realized that maybe I didn't care so much about what other people thought about me after all. Cos if all you were ever trying to do was impress other people you'd never be happy. Not really.

But, hey, don't get me wrong. I'll probably still be ridiculously famous. With this much talent, it's not like I've got a choice, right? But maybe I needed it a little less than I did a month ago. And that ain't no bad thing.

'Maybe I'll put it online tomorrow,' I said to Umer. 'Or the next day. No rush.'

'Sounds good,' said Umer, smiling.

'Right now though,' I said, turning to face them, 'I got something more important to do.'

'What's that?' asked Wendy.

'Beat you two suckers to the other side of the pond!' I replied.

And, with that, I turned and ran as fast as I could towards the stepping stones. The others laughed and chased after me. I knew already it was gonna be a good summer.

Grandpa and Auntie Uzma were hosting the family dinner that weekend, and all the usual gang showed up. Aunts, uncles and cousins crowded round the table. I gotta tell you, I was pleased to see everyone bring a bit less food than they had a month ago. I never thought I'd be a healthy eater, but I had a whole new appreciation of salad. As long as it had been checked for slugs, that is . . .

'Oh, no, no, no,' said Uncle Bashir, refusing Auntie Uzma's bowl of butter chicken. 'I'm on a diet.

I have put on two stone this year.'

Everyone turned to Auntie Uzma, waiting for her to give him a hard time.

'What?' said Uzma. 'No argument here. I am on a diet too.'

After that, no one had another bite. A couple of months like this and we might finally get back to our usual slightly out-of-shape shapes.

Later, while the kids all played and the grown-ups all talked, I sat down in the corner of the living room with Grandpa.

'Have you had a chance to think about what they asked you?' he said.

'Who, the Agency?' I replied.

Grandpa nodded.

'Yeah, course. I ain't been able to think about much else.'

'Whatever you decide, *that* is the right choice,' he said, putting his arm round my shoulder.

He didn't ask me anything more about it after that.

'What about you? What are you going to do next?' I asked him.

'I shall take your auntie to Peru,' he said with a grin.

He was staring over to the far side of the living room, where Auntie Uzma was sitting with a purring David Chesterton in her lap. She and Mum were flicking their way through a travel catalogue called 'Peruvian Paradise'.

'I have been too sleepy,' said Grandpa. 'Not paid enough attention. Time to put that right.'

'I think that sounds like a good plan, Uncle,' I told him.

'And then, when I am back,' he added, 'maybe you can come and visit and I will teach you magic trick number two?'

'Yeah, I'd like that,' I replied. 'I'd like that a lot.'

It was still light outside when Mum and Dad drove me home that evening. Man, I love summer. And, even though Dad was driving, it was a pretty smooth journey. I can't put my finger on it exactly, but something had changed. I knew that neither of them could remember a thing about what had happened. About the cricket or the after-school job, or, you know, the whole alien invasion bit.

Everything that had taken place since that first day with Mustafa and Miss Crumble had been erased. Umer, Wendy, Grandpa and I were the only ones in Eggington who remembered any of it.

Yet somehow, deep inside the rest of them, I think something of that time had remained.

Yeah, my dad was still hot-headed and prone to exaggeration – and I'm pretty sure he'd still send me to live in Pakistan at the drop of a hat. But for some reason I couldn't place, I knew I'd got through to him. He wasn't making stuff up so much any more. He wasn't getting nearly so angry. And most importantly, at that particular moment, he wasn't driving like he wanted to kill us all.

Mum was still the same though. Twice as clever as me and three times as clever as Dad. Still, a few times that night, while I'd sat talking with Grandpa, I'd caught her smiling at me from across the room. I reckon that's all she had wanted. For me to appreciate my family. And, as luck would have it, there's nothing in the world quite like an alien slug invasion to make you appreciate your loved ones. Turns out mine weren't so bad after all.

So that's pretty much it. That's my story. I know some of you will say I made it up, but that's OK – I'm used to it. I *do* make a lot of stuff up. Whether you believed it or not, I hope you enjoyed it.

And, whatever the case, I promised those Agency

guys I wouldn't tell anyone about the whole alien invasion thing, so best keep it to yourself, yeah? I wouldn't want to get in trouble and lose my job.

. . . Oh, did I forget to mention that? That's what they wanted to talk to me about at the doctor's. Turns out they'd been looking to recruit some fresh blood since my uncle had retired. I guess I'm not going to be a ninja-rapper-gangster after all.

I'm going to be a ninja-rapper-secret-agent.

I can live with that.

DISAPPEARING
COIN TRICK!

**OK, just like I promised,
here's the secret to Grandpa's amazing
coin trick! Get practising!**

1 Right, so first up, hold the
coin between your thumb and
forefinger like this, yeah?

2 Next, reach in like you're
gonna take it with the other
hand – but really just cover it
up so the audience can't see.

3 Once it's hidden from view, let it drop into your palm. Then, really carefully, hide the coin in your pocket — but you have to be sneaky cos you don't want anyone to see you doing it!

4 Make a fist with your other hand. Hold up your fist and blow on it.

5 And TA-DA! Open your hands to reveal the coin has vanished!

There you go! Now you're a magician too. Remember not to tell anyone!

ACKNOWLEDGEMENTS

Firstly, a big thank-you to our lovely aunties, who've never once tried to murder us or take over the world. A huge thanks to our mums – for all the obvious mum stuff – but also for being first-draft readers and early note-givers. And, of course, a big thanks to our dads, for allowing us years of research into the field of crazy, shouting dads. It would be a different book without you.

Massive thanks to Humza's manager, Dhanny Joshi, and agent, Matilda Forbes-Watson, for all your hard work getting this book off the ground. And to Henry's agent, Sean Gascoine, for all your help over the years and for supporting me in trying something new (and to Hannah Begbie for the first leg). Thanks to Sam Bryant who first introduced us and kicked off this creative partnership. Thanks to

Andy Siddons for always being there to read drafts and offer thoughts.

A special thanks to our editors, Holly Harris and Sharan Matharu, for all their incredible work and support throughout this process. Fanks to Shreeta Shah four picking up are million litle errors and putting them wright ;-) Thanks to Roz Hutchison for telling the world about our funny little story. And to all the rest of the amazing team at Puffin Books who have helped get this book polished up and ready to go – thanks a million. Plus, of course, a great big well-inked and shockingly shaded thank-you to Aleksei Bitskoff for his awesome artwork.

And, finally, thanks to all the kids who read this when they could have been playing video games.

 **Humza Arshad** is one of the UK's most popular and important British Asian personalities. After graduating from Richmond Drama School, Arshad wrote, directed and edited the first episode of his online series, *Diary of a Badman*. Over 80 million views of the series later, Humza became the first British YouTuber to have his own scripted comedy series on BBC Three in the mockumentary series *Coconut*. Equally important to Humza has been using his influence and comedy for a greater purpose. In 2015 Humza partnered with the UK Counter Terrorism Unit and he is YouTube's first ambassador for the Creators For Change campaign. Humza has spoken and shared the stage with the likes of Will Smith, YouTube CEO Susan Wojcicki, Kevin Hart and Whoopi Goldberg.

Follow Humza on Twitter, Snapchat and Instagram
@HumzaProduction

and on YouTube
@HumzaProductions

 **Henry White** is a comedy writer working in television and children's fiction. He grew up in west London and began his career in online animation. Henry went on to write and direct adverts for a number of British comedy channels, before working as a sitcom writer. He has a birthmark shaped like a duck.

THE BEGINNING

Wait – you didn't think that was it, did you?

Puffin has **LOADS** more stories for you to discover.

Find your next adventure at **puffin.co.uk**, along with:

- **Quizzes, games and apps starring your favourite characters**
- **Videos, podcasts and audiobook extracts**
- **The chance to check out brand-new books before anybody else!**

puffin.co.uk

Psst! You can also find Puffin on PopJam